Alabaster

"Imaginative, authentic, and evocative.
A powerful narrative beautifully told."

Gerard Kelly, author of
The Boy Who Loved Rain

Chris Aslan has spent many years living in Central Asia. Chris wrote a part memoir, part travelogue called, *A Carpet Ride to Khiva: Seven years on the Silk Road*, about life in Uzbekistan and is currently lecturing on textiles, tour-guiding around Central Asia and studying in Oxford for Anglican ordination. Chris's website is www.chrisaslan.info.

Alabaster

Chris Aslan

LION FICTION

Published by Lion Fiction
an imprint of
Lion Hudson plc
Wilkinson House, Jordan Hill Road
Oxford OX2 8DR, England
www.lionhudson.com/fiction

ISBN 978 1 78264 228 2
e-ISBN 978 1 78264 229 9

First edition 2016

A catalogue record for this book is available from the British Library

Printed and bound in the UK, October 2016, LH26

*For my own sisters, Helen and
Sheona, and for Aksana, Gulnora
Opa, and my other sisters in
Central Asia.*

I still hear the voice of my mother telling me what all women in our village tell their daughters: "Mariam, a woman's honour is as fragile and as beautiful as a butterfly's wings. What is a butterfly without wings, except a worm? Remember this. Guard your reputation, for it is more precious even than a husband or sons."

It's probably a good thing that my mother didn't live to see me now.

Chapter One

I'm floating on a sea of sand, buffeted and thrown by sand waves, and now I've got sand in my mouth and I'm choking, trying not to drown. I wake up coughing as dust and debris rain down from above.

The ground is heaving and juddering beneath us, and I can hear the roof beams creaking overhead and the walls and packed-earth floor splitting and cracking. My mother-in-law and sister-in-law scream. Dried mud and debris from the ceiling cover us and then one of the screams is cut short and turns into a spasm of choking. Someone must have mud in their lungs.

Something sharp strikes my temple and I cry out. If I hadn't realized before, now I know that this isn't a dream; it's real. I try to burrow under the bedding to shield myself. As I do, my husband, Ishmael, lunges from his place on the mat beside me, crying out to his mother. From her sudden sob of relief I know she now clings to him and that he shields her from the falling debris, a hand probably stretching out for his choking sister. I'm left alone on the mat. Blood, warm and slick, dribbles like wax down my temple.

The ground stops shaking. Soon there is only the sound of sobbing and panting and the muffled panic of the livestock in their stable which shares a wall with our inner room. We all yelp as the ground jerks again, as if it's playing with us and just wanted to lull us into a false sense of security. Then the earth is still once more. Gradually, our heartbeats steady and our breaths become more regular.

"Mariam, don't just sit there; light a lamp!" my mother-in-law snaps. I feel for the wall at the head of my mat and fumble along it until my fingers reach the alcove and curl around a squat clay oil lamp. Keeping my hand to the wall, I edge along, stifling a cry as my bare feet step on something sharp. I feel my way to the door that leads outside to our kitchen area. I have to yank at the door, which has got stuck, and when it comes loose it hangs at a funny angle.

Outside, the stars shine brightly, giving just enough light to see. The moon has already set, so it must be the last watch of the night and close to dawn. The embers from last night's fire have died out. It takes me longer to find the flint and kindle a flame. I toss on a few extra sticks while I fill the lamp with olive oil and twist a new wick which I lay in its spout before lighting it. "Mariam!" I hear my mother-in-law cry out sharply, and hurry back inside. The family are huddled together in a nest of blankets. Shoshanna rocks her daughter, Rivka, as if she were a baby, although she is thirteen and only two years younger than me.

"Is everyone alright?" Ishmael asks. His concerned gaze does not include me. I brush at some hair that has got caught in the clotting blood from my temple. They nod, wide-eyed. Then Shoshanna rouses herself. "We must check the livestock. Mariam?" I make for the lower room where we keep the animals. "No! Light another lamp first. Don't leave us in the dark." I bring the lamp over to her. Its light makes her plump features seem unusually hollow. "And wash your face," she adds, a little more gently. "You're bleeding." The lamplight throws the new cracks on the walls into relief. Ishmael only plastered the walls last summer and now he'll have to do it all over again.

I go back to the kitchen porch and add another few sticks to the fire, before lighting another lamp and checking on the stable. I'm greeted with expectant bleats, although I haven't brought any fodder. The sheep and goats seem fine. Any debris that fell from the ceiling has disappeared into the straw, and you can't even tell that the earthquake happened.

Not so outside. I hear panicked voices and the occasional shriek from further down the street, and a stab of fear pierces my heart.

I hurry back inside. "Auntie," I say, keeping my head bowed and using the respectful form of address. "With your permission, may I visit my sister to make sure she is unharmed?"

"And leave us to clean up all this mess?" Rivka pouts.

"It will be easier for me to clean in daylight," I add, cursing Rivka silently.

Shoshanna cocks her head and hears all the noise outside. It won't be improper for a woman to be walking alone at night, given the circumstances. She gives me a curt nod, and then Ishmael gives me that look, and we both know that I will be back before sunrise or I will pay for it.

"Cover yourself," Shoshanna adds, never one to let an earthquake stand in the way of decorum. I cover my head, grab my cloak, pull on my sandals and slip out of our walled compound. The village is dotted with lamp-glow as if it were a feast day. My sister lives on the other side of our village, which isn't large. As I make my way along the street, carefully avoiding a tethered donkey bucking against its rope, I make a mental inventory of loss based on the sounds that drift from each compound. I hear the keening cry of mourning coming from Yakob's household, and I'm guessing someone was fatally hit by debris. I'll come and wail myself tomorrow, but not until I know if Marta is alright. Most families are dragging their bedding out into their walled compounds or up onto their flat roofs, in case there are more tremors to come. There are plenty of people on the streets, and shouts of relief as relatives and neighbours discover each other alive.

I keep my head down and no one greets me – not that anyone would. The spring rains have come and the paths are muddy. I try to keep near the walls where it's drier and get a fright when I almost step on a roosting chicken. She squawks. I hurry on past the well, which is the centre of our village, squared by shops and date palms. As I pass my former friend Imma's house, I'm tempted to stop and enquire about their safety, even if she hates me. Then I hear her father, Halfai, break into a holy song of thanks in his quavering, tuneless voice, and I know their family has survived unscathed.

I'm breathless as I'm heading uphill. Our house is on the uppermost edge of the village and I can already smell the apricot blossom from our tree. I reach the rise towards the olive hills and clamber up the rocks where Eleazar once slipped and fell while we were playing and lay unconscious as I ran home shrieking that I'd committed murder. A little further and I've reached home. Above are the stretching branches of the apricot tree that dominates our small, walled compound. There's no time to breathe in their delicate, heady scent. I need to know that my sister is alive.

The outside door is bolted and there is no light coming from inside. Fear roils in the pit of my stomach and I can taste bile at the back of my throat. I don't even bother banging on the door, but hitch up my cloak and tunic, take a run at the wall and grab one of the overhanging boughs dimly visible. I haul myself up. I can feel the bruises on my ribs from my last beating, but ignore them and scrabble my legs up and then over.

Undignified, I drop into our compound and almost trip over the warp threads of Marta's latest carpet, staked out beneath the shade of the apricot blossom. I barely have time to wonder why she's started on a carpet this early in the year when it's too damp to be hunched over a loom.

"Marta?" I call, and duck into the outdoor covered kitchen area, wishing I'd brought a lamp with me. There are still some

glowing embers in the hearth, which means Marta must have worked late and eaten even later. I light a lamp and hurry inside, slipping off my sandals at the threshold. She's huddled against the wall underneath the alcove of two shelves beside our mother's dowry chest with her feet drawn up, clutching a treasure to her bosom. I breathe out a slow sigh of relief.

Marta looks up, deep circles beneath her eyes. Her gaze falls upon my bare feet. "You shouldn't have bothered taking off your sandals," she says, dully. "Look at the place. It'll take me all morning just to sweep it clean."

"Marta!" I run over to her, placing the lamp in the alcove. She says nothing for a moment; her chest is heaving. I lean against the wall. Relief that she's unharmed floods through me and I sink down beside her and kiss her cheek.

"It's safe," she says, and lifts the object that she cradles between her breasts, as if to show me a newborn. It is the head of an exquisite jar made from alabaster. It is our most precious possession and also our curse.

"Why did you take out the jar?" I ask. "Did something fall onto the dowry chest during the earthquake?"

"It wasn't in the chest during the earthquake," she says. Her voice is flat.

She slaps her face hard with one hand, the other keeping a careful grasp of the jar.

"Marta!" I say. She hits her face again, this time with a fist, and is about to hit herself a third time before I grab her wrist. "What has possessed you?" I ask. There's enough hitting in my life already. She says nothing and we sit silently for a while.

"I took it out two nights ago," she eventually explains. "I just held it in my hands, and oiled it a bit to burnish the alabaster." She tails off for a moment. "Each night I put it up on that shelf and put a lamp beside it and just watched it until I fell asleep. I probably sound like some kind of idolatrous unbeliever, but I just wanted to remind myself to hope."

"Of course," I say, holding her tight and trying to sound as if I understand and don't think she's going crazy. "But what were you thinking, displaying it so openly? What if someone had seen it?"

"I know," she says sharply "I know," softer this time. "When the quaking started, I jumped up straightaway. I knew exactly what was happening and wondered if this was the punishment of God for putting my trust in the jar. I leapt for the shelf. The jar had already fallen on its side. A moment later and it would have rolled and crashed into pieces at my feet. Can you imagine?" She is wide-eyed and grips my shoulder tightly.

"Is it damaged?"

She gently passes the jar over to me. I take it in my hands. Its heft, its weight and its beauty are so familiar to me. The alabaster has been warmed by her body. I gaze at the mottled, translucent surface. How many times have I done this? I used to imagine I saw meaning or even glimpses of the future in the swirls and shapes of this stone, more polished even than marble. Of course, it means nothing.

"Pass me the lamp," I say, and Marta, understanding my intent, raises it a little to cast more light as I trace my fingers over the curved cylinder of the jar, probing for cracks or fissures. It feels smooth to the touch, except for the bands of etched patterns around the top of the jar, which are all as they should be.

The alabaster is translucent and it's only when I lift the jar and hold it against the lamplight that I see a crack has worked itself along one side. The surface is still completely smooth and I realize that the crack must be inside, where the perfume is.

"No one will notice it in daylight," I say, laughing a little with relief. "It's still just as valuable." She says nothing. I continue to study the surface of the jar, spitting on one section and rubbing it with the hem of my tunic. No one in my village has ever seen anything like it and none of them know that we have it. It's our secret. The jar is full of almost one pint of pure spikenard and it's worth a fortune. I don't even know what spikenard smells like,

Chris Aslan

although that's never stopped my imagination. This recipient of all our hopes and dreams almost shattered. I hug the jar to me, and it's as if Marta can read my thoughts.

"How could I have been so stupid, so careless?" she says. She looks up at me. Her skin looks gaunt and sallow; her beautiful curls are lank and uncared-for. "Miri, I don't think I can carry on like this for much longer," she says. I'm holding my breath. I've never heard her speak like this before. "I keep asking myself if this is all there is, or if it will get better."

"Of course things will get better," I say, trying to sound hopeful. "You could start training some weaving apprentices. We could even sell the jar. That would give you enough coinage to open a whole workshop!" I'm pleased with this idea, but Marta looks stung and hurt.

"You think I would part with the jar for a workshop?" she asks. "You mean that I should give up all hope of marriage?"

"That's not what — "

"A withered old raisin someone forgot to harvest — who could possibly want her? Eh? I should let the whole village know about the jar and then we'll see about suitors."

I match her short, bitter laugh with one of my own. "Trust me, that is not what you want."

"Are they treating you badly?" Marta asks, rousing herself and stroking my cheek. And just like that, she is transformed back into her usual role of older sister; the comforter, not the comforted.

"I'm fine," I lie. I don't want her to worry. Anyway, what could she do? "I'm glad he doesn't know about this," I say. "It's one thing he will never get his hands on."

"Here, let me put it back in the chest out of harm's way." She opens the chest and holds the jar tenderly for a moment before burying it at the bottom of the robes, headscarves, tunics, and other remnants of our mother's dowry.

"Do you ever think about how Father got it?" Marta asks.

"Not any more," I lie again. "Does it really matter now?"

13

Alabaster

It's a secret I carry alone and one she'll never know. I think about it all the time; sometimes I'm left merely heartbroken and other times I have a raging desire to smash the cursed jar and to scratch out the eyes of God with its shards.

It was two years after Mother died and Father had just begun to learn to smile again. I had nothing to smile about: Marta had asked me to help her sift through a whole sack of dry lentils, taking a bowlful at a time and spreading them out on white cloth to spot and remove little stones. "They could easily end up costing you a tooth," she'd warned. It was a job I neither enjoyed nor excelled in, but Marta had decided I needed training in the wifely skills of homemaking. Eleazar sat in the shade of the apricot tree working on his letters, not doing very well. Happy for the excuse to help him, I went over to read with him, but ended up being impatient and then laughing.

"What help would I need from you?" he spat. He always reminded me of a hissing kitten when he got cross, and I just laughed again. "What does a girl know of reading? Might as well teach a donkey the alphabet." This was no longer funny. I grabbed at him but he wriggled away and was up the tree and over the wall in a moment.

"Father, did you hear that?" I asked as he emerged from the unclean place in one corner of our compound.

Father sighed. "Could you pour water for me?" He soaped his hands, squatting beside the fragrant herbs Marta had planted next to the unclean place to mask its smell, while I poured water over his hands from a jug. It was still early in the day but already the heat was palpable.

"Come on," he said. "We need to separate you two. You come with me to water the saplings, and Eleazar can stay here with Marta."

"You mean, we should work while Eleazar goes off swimming all day?"

Father said nothing, but managed to sigh, smile ruefully and

Chris Aslan

look up at me with his large brown eyes, and I was mollified. I knew Father was worried that the heat would bring on one of the summer fevers which had killed Mother and still sometimes affected my brother. Marta just looked up, shook her head at me in absent-minded despair and lost herself in her lentils again.

Later, as we trudged up the slope of the olive hill towards our grove, I was still unwilling to let the matter drop. "It's not fair. I managed to learn letters much faster than him when I was his age. Even if I don't understand the holy language much, why should he get to sit at Holy Halfai's feet and not me?"

Father smiled. The donkey panted between us, heavily laden with two large, seeping water-skins strapped on either flank. Father adjusted one of the leather straps. "You shouldn't call Halfai that," he said. "It's not respectful."

"But why shouldn't I study?"

"I didn't make the rules," said Father.

"Yes, but still…"

Father ran a hand over his brow and his face, drawing the sweat down his beard and then wiping his hand on his light robe, which was already clinging under his arms. I liked his smell because it was his, even if it was a little strong that day. My father was a master at speaking without words and this simple gesture managed to convey: "It is hot, we still have a way to go before we reach the grove, and there's nothing I can do to change the situation. How will further fights help?"

We walked on without speaking, our panting blending with the donkey's rasp against a background hum of cicadas. My hair was damp under my headscarf and I could feel rivulets of sweat beneath my tunic dribble all the way down my back and into the crevice of my buttocks. Although our house was at the top of the village, nearest the olive hills, our land was also furthest away and it was midday before we arrived there.

There was no obvious border, but we both knew exactly where our land started. I think olive trees are like clusters of women at

15

a well. A stranger to our village would see only women in shabby robes, tunics and headscarves, water jars balanced on their heads or tucked into the crook of a shoulder. Me? I know each one of them. I know who has patched her robe well or badly, the gait and preferred carrying stance of each individual, the shape of each figure – even beneath their robes – and that's before they even turn around and I can see their face. It's the same with our trees. I may forget the ages of the oldest trees but I can tell you which prophets were alive when they were mere saplings. Each is different, whether a slim and graceful sapling or a squat, swarthy ancient. I know each bulge, each severed limb, the holes where owls roost, their twists and turns, which ones give the best olives. Each is like a woman from the village. They could all survive a whole summer of drought, except for the row of saplings Father planted last year up on the rocky bluff in front of the ravine. This was where we were heading.

As we passed the largest of the olive trees, I spotted what looked like a large pile of discarded rags under it.

"Someone's left their old clothes here," I said.

Father's brow furrowed.

"Wait here with the donkey." He handed me the rope and went nearer. The rag pile moved slightly and moaned.

The donkey sank down to the ground, exhausted. I knew we'd have a job getting him back up again. I dropped the rope, following behind Father.

"Are you hurt?" Father asked, bending down to the pile. There was another moan and I leaned over Father's shoulder. We could tell from the ragged turban that this must be a man, but the end of it covered his face, so we couldn't see anything more. Father lifted it and we both recoiled in horror.

He looked like a man made from the oldest of olive trees. Instead of skin, he was covered in brown, cracking and fissuring bark. His face bulged with growths in unexpected places, the largest above his left eye, swelling it shut and making it look as

Chris Aslan

if that side of his face was made of wax and had melted. Where his nose should have been there was a stump out of which oozed something resembling sap.

I gagged but managed not to vomit.

"I'm sorry," the olive man managed to whisper. It clearly took effort to speak, as if the insides of his throat had also turned to bark. He fixed his one remaining eye, milky blue with cataract, on Father. "Is this your land?"

Father swallowed, and when he spoke his voice was strained. "Yes, it is. You're welcome to rest here."

A raspy sound came from the man's throat, which might even have been laughter. Whatever it was, it dissolved into a bout of weak coughing and he panted and rasped, trying to get more air.

"Mariam, what are you standing there for? Fetch our guest some water," said Father. I hurried back to the donkey and untied the small leather skin filled with well water rather than water from the brook, and carried it over to Father. He cradled the man's head, lifting it so that he could pour a trickle of water down the man's throat. I recoiled at the foul, rotting stench coming from his mouth, but Father didn't seem to notice.

"Mariam, step back. Give our guest some space," said Father, although I was already keeping my distance. It took time for the man to be sated, as he was only able to drink a little at a time. Eventually he waved his hand feebly and Father stopped.

"Thank you," rasped the man. "I am sorry to have inconvenienced you."

"Are you sick?" I asked, realizing how stupid the question was as soon as I asked it. "Father, I could run back to the village and call on Aunt Shiphra. She might have a balm or something."

"No. There is no need. It is far too late for that."

My eyes widened, and I tried to mouth silently to Father: "*Is he a leper?*" Father gave an almost imperceptible nod and then turned to the leper whose head he cradled.

"What is your name?"

17

Alabaster

"Name?" The leper seemed puzzled. "I have lost much but that was one of the first things to go. Names are for people."

"Would you like some food? I apologize, we seem to have forgotten our manners," said Father, and I turned to fetch some bread and cheese from the saddlebags.

The leper wheezed and shook his head. "It is too late for that, too," he said. "I can't eat any more."

"Is there anything I can do?" Father asked, his voice catching with emotion.

"Do you sing?" asked the leper. "*For I have eaten ashes like bread, and mingled my drink with weeping.*"

Father recognized the holy song and began it at the beginning, his voice deep and sorrowful.

I drew closer but Father shook his head and waved in the direction of the donkey. I walked back and listened as Father sang. Once he had finished one holy song, he began another, rocking the man's head tenderly. He was interrupted briefly when the leper had another coughing fit and again when the donkey brayed because I was forcing him to his feet.

I dragged the donkey up to the ridge, keeping away from the ravine on the other side, and found some dried scrub for him to graze. Loosening the leg of one of the water-skins, made of an entire goat, I poured water into a small clay jar and then tied the skin shut and watered the nearest sapling.

I kept this up into the afternoon, and soon my tunic clung to me with spilled water and sweat. All the time I could hear Father's voice drifting up. It was too hot to think and it was only when the last of the water had been poured onto the last sapling and I'd dragged the donkey under the shade of the nearest tree that I began to consider our predicament. I didn't know much about the law but I knew that it was illegal to bring a leper into the village, and that we were now sullied and would need to wash ourselves completely before we could return home. I also knew that lepers were dangerous and that their disease was contagious. I wondered how long Father had been sitting beside this diseased man and whether he would be infected.

Fear clutched at my heart and I hurried back to the large tree, following Father's voice. He had taken his linen shawl and tied it to the overhanging boughs to give further shade. The leper seemed to sleep. Father looked up and although his voice did not waver, I saw tears coursing down his cheeks. He sang until he had finished the last line of the holy song, and then he said quietly, "He is gone, Mariam. I think his last breath was during the song before this one."

"Oh, Father," I cried, and rushed towards him.

"No," he said sharply. "Keep back."

I stayed where I was as Father gently laid the head to rest on the earth and eased himself out from under it. "What do we do now?" I asked.

"We spoke," he said. "In between the singing, there were things he needed to tell me."

"Like what?" I asked.

"Much was only for my ears. He knew that we could not leave his body on our land. Not with the sickness still within it."

I looked up at the row of saplings. "Together we could drag him up to the ridge and then roll him into the ravine."

"No, there must be a better way."

"Like what? We won't be allowed to bring the body into the village or to any of the tombs, and anyway, it's too far and the donkey is exhausted."

Father thought for a moment. "I don't want you coming near the body or touching it," he said. Untie the water-skins and we'll see if between me and the donkey we can drag the body up to the ridge."

As it turned out, under all those rags, the leper was so shrunk and desiccated that soon the donkey was dragging the corpse behind him, Father lifting the body where he could, as if worried at its discomfort. At the ridge we paused and Father sang prayers

over the leper before he rolled him over and we watched the
bundle of rags tumbling and bouncing down the ravine until it
came to a halt behind one of the larger boulders.

"It doesn't feel right," said Father quietly.

"You sang for him, Father, in his last hour," I said.

"At least his suffering has ended," Father muttered. He picked
up the ropes and led the donkey back to the large olive tree so we
could collect the empty water-skins.

"What should we do with his staff and his bell and his bag?" I
asked. They still lay in a bundle under the olive tree.

"Don't touch anything," said Father, stretching into the
branches to untie his linen cloak. "It is all sullied."

He picked up the bell and the staff and the bag and nimbly
climbed back up to the ridge, where I saw him throw them into
the ravine. This gave just enough time for the thought I had been
batting away like a persistent mosquito to land and settle: *Father, if
it's sullied, then why are you touching it, and what if you catch this disease?*
My stomach felt queasy and I found myself rubbing my hands
against my sweat-soaked tunic as if that would clean them.

When Father came back he was holding something in his
hands. Even though he motioned that I should keep my distance
from him, I could see that it was some kind of container made of
something much finer, more delicate and intricate than anything
of clay or of anything I had ever seen before, even in our house
of prayer.

"What is it?" I asked.

"I'm not sure," said Father. "He said that it was a gift for me,
a token of gratitude."

"Can I hold it?" I was mesmerised by the swirling patterns of
the alabaster, so polished and gleaming it looked more like gold
than stone.

"No. It must be cleansed first." Father slipped it into the
saddlebag and we turned towards the village. We hadn't eaten
midday meal, but Father said that we must leave the bread and

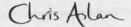

Chris Aslan

cheese behind for the birds, as it might have been tainted by the sickness.

"Thank you for your help with the saplings," he added after a while. "You did the work of a grown man today."

I beamed, because hearing my father's approval was perhaps as precious to me as whatever our bulging saddlebag contained.

"Father," I said as we neared the village, "could we have caught leprosy from the man?"

Father smiled tightly. "If God wills it, but I doubt it. You didn't even come into contact with him."

"I know," I said quietly. "But you did. Why didn't you just leave him? It's not worth the risk, and anyway, we broke the law. You should never have touched him."

Father stopped in his tracks, tugging on the donkey as he did so. "Mariam, look at me. If God allowed this man – not just a leper, but a man – in need to rest on our land, to be our guest, then we have broken no law by treating him with hospitality and kindness. Do you understand me? That is how I've raised you."

I couldn't help it; I started to cry. "But Father, what if I ever lost you?" I blubbed.

Father was about to embrace me but then remembered to keep his distance. "Come now, Mariam, let's have no more of that talk. When we get back to the village, you can go home and collect fresh clothes and soap, and I'll take the donkey straight down to the brook and meet you there. We'll soon be clean again."

I sniffed and wiped my nose on my sleeve.

"Let's say nothing of this to Marta or Eleazar," said Father. "They'll only worry."

"But how will we explain about the jar?"

"We know nothing about the jar ourselves. When we do, we can tell them."

Back at the house, Marta looked hot and fractious and failed to notice my inability to look her in the eye. "It's not enough," I said, as she carefully cut a small nub off our block of olive soap.

21

"It's plenty, Miri. You're not the one who has to make it."

I explained that we were unclean. "We'll have to wash our clothes too. There was a dead body, and we had to move it and throw it into the ravine."

Marta made a face. "What was it? A jackal?"

"Something like that," I said, and turned before she could ask me anything else. The sun was slanted and golden by the time I set out for the brook near the bottom of the village with two sets of clean clothes. I overtook one of the shepherd boys whom my best friend, Imma, had nominated as the best-looking boy in our village.

"Hey, Ishmael, are you going to the brook?" I asked. He nodded. "Could I give you this for my father?"

I passed him soap and clothing, and as we neared the brook I walked towards the tall reeds where women can wash in seclusion. Ishmael spotted our donkey grazing beside the brook in the men's area and headed there.

I dawdled to watch him for a moment. He flexed his shoulder with confidence, shrugging off his clothes, and then looked in my direction as he reached down to slip off his linen waist cloth, as if he knew he had an audience. I ducked away, blushing, and heard the splash as he plunged into the brook.

I stepped out of my sweat-sodden clothes and squatted amongst the reeds, checking over my body for any of the tell-tale white marks that would indicate leprosy, even though I knew it took time before the disease showed itself. I could hear Ishmael and Father talking together. To stop myself thinking about the shepherd, I imagined the jar which Father would carefully remove from the saddlebag and scrub once Ishmael had left. Even back then, I somehow knew that it would change our lives forever, although if I had known what the future held, I would have taken the jar and smashed it against the rocks into a thousand pieces.

Chapter Two

We walk down the street; three mourning women. Our hair and headscarves are grey, covered in flecks of soot and ash, our throats sore from wailing, our eyes puffy from weeping, and our cheeks still red where we've been slapping ourselves.

"Wait," wheezes a voice from behind us as our plump neighbour, Ide, catches up. She limps from her club foot and always seems out of breath. "Have you seen Crazy Mariam?" There are several Mariams in our village, but only one was born crazy. "She managed to get out of their house while Cyria was at the funeral. Cyria checked the street and with the neighbours but no one has seen her."

"How many times has this happened?" Rivka sighs in disgust. "When will that woman learn to lock her daughter up if she has to go out? Do you remember the time they found her naked by the well, wanting to jump in?"

"Rivka!" says Shoshanna, and Rivka rolls her eyes but says no more. "No, we haven't seen her. Poor Cyria."

"May God have mercy," Ide says, tutting her tongue. "Well, we may as well walk back together." What she really means is that

23

she'd like to discuss the funeral and enjoy a good gossip with my mother-in-law. I doubt Crazy Mariam or her mother will get much of a mention, as all the possible sins Cyria could have committed to be cursed with a crazed daughter have been discussed to the point that even these women are bored. I sometimes wonder whether it has ever occurred to Ide that her gossiping friends might be discussing the sins of her own mother for birthing a cripple.

"Poor Marta," Shoshanna shakes her head mournfully. This isn't my Marta she's talking about; it's old Marta, Yakob's wife, who was struck fatally by a falling beam during the earthquake last night.

"Do you remember what a beauty she was when we were young girls?" says Ide, and they both smile. "She could walk to the well with her water jug on her shoulder wearing a faded old robe, but when those hips swayed, half the men in the village petitioned their mothers for a match. Hah!"

"It will be hard for old Yakob. Marta always thought he'd be the first to go," said Shoshanna. "Thank God she was the only fatality last night."

"Did the earthquake reach the city?" asks Rivka, which I have to admit is a good question. Although our village is small and conservative, it only takes half a day by donkey to reach our cosmopolitan, walled capital. I've never been, but I've heard about it from my cousin Lukas. I expect their huge stone buildings barely creaked, but what do I know? Rivka's question is ignored. More important for the two neighbours is the correct apportioning of blame for Marta's death last night.

"I wonder why she was singled out. Was there something she did that none of us knew about?" says Ide.

"I'm sure that hers was not a wandering eye, at least not in old age," says Shoshanna, and they both savour the possibility that in her hip-swaying days this might not have been the case.

"Did you notice anything unusual about her?" says Ide, and they begin a tedious inventory of potential sin.

"Of course, it could be that God wishes to punish Yakob by smiting his wife," Rivka adds, bored with the conversation. "Or perhaps it was one of Marta's children who sinned?"

This opens several potential new lines of enquiry, but by now we've reached home. Ide is clearly waiting for an invitation to join us. Shoshanna is about to ask her in, when Rivka interrupts, saying, "I'm exhausted; first the earthquake and all that clearing up, and then the funeral. I'm sure you must be tired, too, Aunt Ide."

"Yes, yes, of course," says Ide, crestfallen, and heads further up the street to her own compound.

At least once a day I picture Rivka dying or me killing her. In the fantasy that now flits through my mind, Rivka tosses her head and marches into the inner room and then the entire house collapses on her and, just like that, she's no more. Of course, I say nothing, even though I was the one who did all the sweeping before dawn. Shoshanna also knows not to antagonize her daughter. Rivka has such a propensity for malice that she would even allow her family to be shamed if it meant wounding someone she hated. And she knows everything and could ruin what little reputation I have left, forever. We both try not to get on the bad side of her. We are held hostage by our secrets.

"Mariam, you must be exhausted," says Shoshanna, yawning. "Rivka will prepare midday meal."

I light a lamp and close the door of our windowless inner room, muffling the angry clatter in the kitchen porch outside where, for once, Rivka is actually being made to work. I unfold a sleeping mat from their pile on top of the chest and lie down, curl up and remember my worst funeral.

Mother had laboured with the fever for four days. Marta and Father took turns to sit by her bedside, and they moved her out of the inner room to the covered kitchen porch area. "Please, I want to see the sky," she had said when she was still lucid on that first day. She went from sweating and arching her back in feverish pain, to shivering and shaking in her drenched bedding. We took it in turns to lie down beside her during the shivers, warming her with our bodies, and then wiping her down with inner-gourds dipped in cool well water during the fevers.

Aunt Shiphra came and went, bringing salves of honey and mashed ginger and cleansing bowls of hyssop water. Our neighbours were also kind to us. The men offered up prayers at the prayer house and the women cooked extra portions and brought them round.

I should have realized when they started lighting lamps at her head and her feet and reciting holy songs that Mother was dying. I was asleep at the end when she stopped breathing. "You were exhausted, and I didn't want to wake you," Marta said tenderly, when I awoke the next day to the sound of my aunt's keening. Marta's face was as ashen and drawn as the corpse beside us. She held me and stroked my hair as I wept, and then circled her arms around me when I threw myself on Mother's cold and stiffening body. Father just sat staring at nothing. I could hear Eleazar laughing next door where he'd been taken to keep him distracted. He still didn't know what had happened.

It was Marta who called on Holy Halfai to come and read over Mother. Aunt Shiphra and the neighbours helped organize food for the mourners and Halfai, whatever I might think of him now, organized everything else. He didn't ask for any money upfront, realizing Father was incapacitated with grief, and procured enough salt for Mother's body to be laid upon, as well as the linen shroud, and the oils and spices needed to prepare Mother's body.

Marta insisted on washing the body herself, even though Shiphra and others offered. I remember it all through a blur of tears, somehow feeling numb and also as if my heart would tear inside me because of the pain, all at the same time. I rocked and wailed with the other women of the village, and tore my favourite robe, tearing out clumps of my hair and slapping myself until my face bruised. The physical pain felt good and when I scratched my

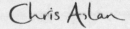

arms and blood came out, it felt as if I'd found a way of letting the pain out. In the end some neighbours had to restrain me from going further.

The men knocked on the compound door with a bier, having come for the body. I flung myself over the shrouded corpse, who until yesterday had been my rock. "No, you can't have her," I screamed, and the neighbour ladies had to restrain me, never holding it against me that I bit, punched, scratched and swore at them as I writhed to escape.

Marta stood up suddenly as if she, too, would launch herself as the bier was carried out of the compound door, but instead she collapsed in a heap and soon the women were fussing around her, calling on each other to give her space, fanning her and offering sips of water.

It never occurred to me that the kindness of these same women might translate into gossip and speculation over my mother's character and God's punishment once they had left our home and were free to talk.

Thankfully, I can hardly remember the next few weeks. I know that Father took us all to see the tombs out on the barren hill; caves in the sand and rock. Marta explained to me and Eleazar that our family tomb had been sealed with mud and rocks but that we would come back next year, unwrap the shroud and place Mother's bones into an ossuary to rest with our grandparents.

I remember that Father seemed dead inside, even though he still breathed and walked and went about his daily tasks. It was Marta who cared for me and Eleazar. She tried to sing us the lullabies Mother used to sing, or make our favourite dishes, but this just made us cry, so she stopped. I never saw her cry in front of us, although she remained gaunt and I don't think she slept much.

One night I woke determined to ignore my need to relieve myself, but eventually crept outside. Lamplight spilled from behind the dusty curtain that screened off the unclean place and I could see the bent silhouette of my sister holding her stomach as if it cramped. She sobbed as quietly as she could. I squatted beside the apricot tree, reasoning that she'd rather I pass water there than interrupt her private grief.

Mother's only brother, an uncle I'd never met, came to mark the fortieth day of mourning, bringing his son Lukas with him. Lukas sat on an extravagant saddle like some sort of prince, with his father walking beside him. It was only once they were inside our compound and Uncle Yosef lifted him down that I realized that Lukas was a cripple. "Careful of my clothes," said Lukas, as we prepared cushions and a seating mattress for him. "It's cotton, from India," he added to me, as I touched the hem of his soft, white robe. I'd never seen cotton before, as we grew our own flax and had our own sheep in our village, and I had no idea of the place he talked of. I helped Marta prepare platters of lamb, cheese and fruit for Holy Halfai and the other village elders who had also joined Father in remembering our mother.

"Father, isn't it interesting the way they sit on floor mats and eat from a floor cloth rather than recline at a table?" said Lukas, as the village elders bristled silently. Mother's loom had been cleared away and they were seated under the apricot tree, a state which Lukas also felt the need to comment upon, wondering why we had never completed the upper room. I waited for his father to cuff him for insolence but nothing was said.

After the meal, Uncle Yosef wanted to visit the tomb, leaving Lukas behind to annoy us. Father had explained earlier that Uncle Yosef had left the village to go north, selling dates and olives. This wasn't that uncommon, but Yosef was somewhat of a family disgrace, having chosen to remain there and marry a Westernized wife.

"Of course, living so close to the Great Lake, we would never eat salt fish like you do. We buy them fresh," Lukas explained to Marta, as we stepped over and around him, trying to clean up the detritus left from the feast.

"I think I can finish up here by myself," said Marta irritably, brushing hair from her forehead with the back of her hand. "Mariam, why don't you take Lukas and show him the village?"

"From what I've already seen, that shouldn't take long," said Lukas, pleased with himself.

I saddled our donkey and was soon walking Lukas down to the well.

"There's not much else to see," I shrugged, after we'd walked around the well and Lukas had made several disparaging comments about the stalls around it and the size of our prayer house.

"But what do people do?" asked Lukas. "I mean, there's no place for discussing ideas. There isn't even an arena."

"What need would a cripple have for an arena?" We turned. It was my cousin, Yokkan, Aunt Shiphra's son. He was the same age as me and Lukas, but was already wiry and muscular and had cultivated the beginnings of a decent beard and the overbearing nature of a young man.

"Er, this is my cousin Yokkan, son of my father's sister," I said, wishing Yokkan could be nice for once. "Yokkan, meet my cousin Lukas, son of my mother's brother. It's his first time in our village."

I gave Lukas a pleading look to be quiet but the stupid boy ignored it. "I was just asking Cousin Mariam what people actually do here."

"We work and we pray. We work hard and we pray hard. Do you know anything about work or prayer?"

"Well, I study and I can speak three languages."

"We study the holy language if there is time between work and prayer."

"But what about the world beyond this village? In my town Westerners and locals meet for debate and discussion of ideas. I mean, you're only a day away from the Holy City."

Yokkan stared at Lukas with contempt. "A donkey that makes pilgrimage to the Holy City is still a donkey. A cripple who talks a lot is still a cripple. Talking is for women and men who don't work and pray." He turned without acknowledging me and left.

"Can we go back now?" Lukas asked, and I nodded and then looked away so I wouldn't see Lukas trying not to cry.

"Father warned me it would be like this. 'The village mentality', he called it," said Lukas, as we plodded homeward. "I'm glad we're leaving tomorrow. I only came because Father promised that we could visit the Holy City. It's still full of people like your cousin, but there are Westerners as well."

Lukas and his father left the next day and never came back. We pride ourselves on our hospitality, but we're not very good with strangers in our village.

I thought of Lukas two years later when we were given the jar. I was sure that he would know what material it was made from and, more importantly, what it contained and how much it was worth. I pestered Father about the jar whenever we had a brief moment together alone, which wasn't often.

"I'm not taking it to the capital," he said. "If it's so valuable, then I run a high risk of getting robbed. We'll wait until the olives have fermented and when I take them to the capital I'll make enquiries."

I agreed, reluctantly. "And one more thing, Miri," he added. "Keep checking your skin when you bathe, just to make sure."

"And you?" I asked.

"Everything is fine," he smiled, and I could tell that he meant it.

We didn't talk about the jar again until a few months later as I helped Father with the olive harvest and, surprisingly, so did Marta, who had usually preferred to stay at home. It soon became clear why she was so keen. Annas, son of the widower Yonah, was harvesting his own olives just down from our grove and we started sharing midday meal together. Marta seemed to glow in his presence. Annas was broad with a hearty laugh and an appetite to match, and Marta soon discovered his preference for green olives and sheep cheese, supplying him plentifully with both.

Nor was Marta the only one to be thinking of love. It was just after dawn and I was walking back from the well with my best friend, Imma, when Ishmael came towards us. He was herding his flock but his eyes were not on the sheep. He stared at us brazenly, his gaze fixed as he passed us towards the well, even though he had to turn his head.

"Mind you don't fall in," I called to him, and he finally turned away.

"I can't believe you said that to him," Imma hissed and we both giggled.

"Did you see the way he was staring at us?" I said. "I thought he was supposed to be devout."

"Staring at you, you mean," said Imma. "Oh, those raven eyes and that tall graceful neck!'" she added in a mocking version of a love-struck Ishmael.

"No, he was staring at *you*. Oh, those dark-honey locks and ripe breasts!" I retorted, playfully tugging her hair.

"Stop it!" she squealed as our laughter attracted disapproving glances from the older women back at the well.

"Come on," I said, and we adjusted our water jars and walked off.

"Do you really think he was looking at me?" asked Imma quietly. "I was sure he was staring at you." She turned to me. "He seems so sure of himself and what he wants."

"And he's not the only one," I said, giving her a nudge.

After that day of harvesting, Marta sent Eleazar to the well to fetch water. We could still hear him protesting about women's work from the street outside as I wondered whether gossip about my contact with Ishmael had reached Marta's ears already.

"I need to start teaching you more dishes," said Marta. "I want you to watch carefully how much dried hyssop, sesame seeds and thyme I mix with the olive oil. I'm not going to be around forever, you know." Once mixed, she smoothed the paste expertly over flat rounds of dough which she tossed carefully onto the baking stone, surrounded by glowing embers, where they puffed up and crisped.

"Are you talking about Annas?" I asked. "Has his mother asked officially yet?"

Marta shook her head and tried to suppress her happiness. "No, nothing official and there's no rush. Anyway, it's good for you to learn."

There *was* a bit of a rush, though. Marta was eighteen and most of her friends were already married, and soon people would begin to click their tongues in sympathy at her.

Late afternoon the next day, when Annas came up to our grove, ready to walk back down to the village together, I asked him to accompany Marta and Eleazar, explaining that Father and I still had a little work to do.

"Eleazar, you can run on ahead, if you like, but make sure you wait for us before you get to the village," said Marta, keen to avoid gossip, but excited to have some unchaperoned time with Annas. She cast a grateful look in my direction as they left. Once they were out of earshot, Father looked at me enquiringly.

"We can't wait for the olives to ferment," I said. "Don't you see what's happening between Annas and Marta? His mother could visit any day with a formal request. That jar could pay for her whole dowry."

Father thought for a moment. "Will you be alright continuing the harvest without me for a day?"

I beamed. "Why not go at dawn tomorrow?"

"How will I explain to Marta?" he said.

I thought for a moment. He could take one of Mother's carpets, but the idea of parting with something she had made was unbearable.

"Ishmael has our sheep. Why not take them to the capital and sell them?"

"Usually he does that for me."

"This time you've decided to make a trip. You don't owe him any explanation."

He left at dawn the next morning and didn't return until after we were asleep that night.

At breakfast I gave him a look that said, "Well?" which he returned with a blink and a nod that said, "I'll tell you later. Wait."

"Annas," said Father, as we trudged up towards our groves together. "I have a particularly large tree I wish to harvest tomorrow, and I need someone tall to help me beat the olives out of it. If I loan you Eleazar and Marta for the day, could you come and help me tomorrow?"

"I can help you now," said Annas, but Father insisted on the trade.

Once we'd left the others and arrived at our grove alone, Father turned to me, laughed, and lifted me up, swinging me round and round.

"It's good news, then?" I asked, trying to keep my voice down. "Tell me everything."

"I will, but first there's something I must do." We climbed up to the ravine and looked down at the mouldering pile of rags. A bone or two had been pulled out and gnawed by a jackal or fox, but what little flesh had been on the bones had dried and disappeared. Father began a song of thanksgiving, lifting his hands and eyes to the heavens.

"First I sold the sheep," Father said, once we were seated under an olive tree. "I see now why it's better to let Ishmael take them. He knows people in the market and he gets a better price than I managed. Still, that doesn't matter now. Once I had some coins in my purse, I went to the apothecary street. I started at the cheaper stalls, looking for jars made of alabaster."

"Alabaster?"

"It turns out that's what the jar is made from. There's a whole section of the bazaar selling the jars, full and empty. I found a much smaller, cheaper-looking jar and asked about it. The merchant said it was an alabaster jar of musk. I worked my way up to the more expensive stalls. The merchants could hear from my accent and see from my robe that I wasn't from the city. They tried to shoo me away, but I persisted, explaining that I had a dowry to buy and shaking my bag of coins as if they were gold.

"Eventually I ended up in the largest of the shops, surrounded by shelves and shelves of stuff. I don't even know what it was, but medicines and perfume, all in vials of glass or clay and some even in alabaster jars. My head was dizzy from smelling the scented oils and musk which the trader kept presenting me with. I feigned interest in the small bottles of perfume. 'Which is most costly?' I asked, and the merchant showed me."

"What did it smell like?"

"I don't know how to describe a smell, Miri, but it was amazing. He told me that it was spikenard from the mountains beyond the East – a perilous journey across rivers and deserts which takes over a year to make. I don't know if that was just his sales pitch or if it was true. I couldn't have bought even the smallest bottle with the money from our sheep. Then I asked him, 'Is spikenard what's in those alabaster jars?' I pointed at the larger alabaster jars stacked carefully behind other merchandise. 'No,' said the merchant. 'These jars are too large to hold such a quantity of nard. It would be too expensive. You can tell from the markings and patterns. There is only one large jar of pure spikenard in this shop and I'd never risk putting it on display.' I asked him if I could see it, just so that I could impress my daughter who had never left our village. He looked me over and then unlocked a chest and drew out a jar of pure spikenard. It looked identical to ours!"

"Did he say how much it was worth?"

"I didn't want to ask straightaway, so instead I asked him how the jar opened. 'There is no opening, which only adds to its value,' the merchant said. 'It is like an egg: there is no door in or out and yet it contains a golden treasure.'" I had never seen Father so animated and I laughed at his impression of the merchant's voice.

"What happened next?"

"So I asked him, 'How do you open it? They must have got the nard in there somehow.' The merchant smiled at me indulgently. 'It is a secret which even I do not know. All I can tell you is that the only way to release even one drop of nard is to break the jar.' My eyes must have widened, which was what the merchant was after. 'I know,' he said. 'Impossible to believe! Who could afford such extravagance? A gift for a mighty king. More than a year's wages poured out in such extravagance.' He was happy to boast of the price to an ordinary villager, knowing I would never actually be his client. We talked a little more and then another customer came and I thanked him and left. I waited until I was back on the main street again and then I couldn't contain myself. I just started laughing and thanking God. People must have thought I was mad."

"More than a year's wages?" I flung my arms around Father and we laughed and cried at the same time.

"Miri, do you know what this means?" he asked, holding me and kissing my forehead. "When we sell the jar it will give us more than enough for both your dowries, with enough left over for Eleazar to ask for any girl in the village."

"When are we going to tell Marta about the jar?" I asked, my eyes shining.

Father thought for a moment. "We'll tell her tonight, after Eleazar is asleep. I don't want us to mention this in front of Annas. When he asks for her, let it be for love."

I climbed the olive trees and beat them with a lightness in my spirit; the patter of falling olives seemed like the sound of blessing falling from heaven. We joined the others for midday meal, and even Eleazar noticed that something was up and asked, "Why is everyone so happy?"

Father and I looked away, smiling, not wanting to catch each other's eye. After midday meal, Annas insisted on helping Father with his biggest tree. Father protested that it would be too hot in the heat of the day, but both men were in high spirits and headed off together. I lay down next to Eleazar, who was asleep, but I knew that a nap was impossible. My head was buzzing with Father's news. God had rewarded my father for the kindness he had shown a stranger in need. I imagined what Yokkan or some of the other militants would have done, hounding the dying man off their land rather than risk being defiled or made unclean.

Once Eleazar had woken up, we trudged up to the largest olive tree in our grove. Father and Annas had stripped down to their grubby linen waist cloths, tucking them between their legs to preserve modesty for those below. Marta and I began gathering the olives littered around us. Both men were covered in sweat, leaves and bits of twig. "I know it's early, but I don't think the donkeys can carry more than we've harvested," said Annas, and called over to Eleazar, "How about a swim to cool off?"

Father grinned and nodded and both men swung down from the branches, beaming like boys. Marta offered Annas his robe, averting her eyes modestly. I held up Father's for him to shrug into. "Can you de-leaf me a bit first," he said, and I picked up one of the empty olive sacks and wiped him down.

Eleazar whooped ahead of the group, keen for a swim, and the men walked on together with Annas's donkey, both carrying full shoulder bags of olives. Marta and I followed behind with our own donkey.

"Is everything alright? You've suddenly become very quiet," said Marta.

"Yes, it's fine. I'm just tired," I lied. I wasn't fine at all. I would have to wait until that night, once I was sure everyone else was asleep, before I woke up Father and beckoned him up onto the roof. I hoped lamplight would be enough to put my fears to rest. I had to see his shoulder again. As I'd wiped away the leaves and twigs, I thought I'd seen something on his back, just out of his line of vision. Perhaps it was nothing – I only saw it fleetingly. Perhaps there was a perfectly good explanation for that small, white patch I thought I saw; something that would calm the fear that sat like a stone in the pit of my stomach.

Chapter Three

Muffled and irritated bleating comes from the stable where the sheep and goats are penned in on this sunny spring day. I know how they feel. Today is our weekly holy day and we are expected to rest – even though for me it means more work later. On days like this, our compound never feels big enough. We're all cooped up together with no chores with which to escape interaction. I suspect Marta has forgotten what day it is and is losing herself in her weaving. She's always managed to immerse herself in everyday tasks so completely it's as if she's in a trance. I envy her.

In our compound, Shoshanna is napping inside while the rest of us sit in the shade of the kitchen area. Rivka is braiding her hair. I don't know why; she'll only have to undo each braid before Shoshanna wakes up, otherwise she'll get an earful about fallen women and stoning.

I'm helping my husband learn by heart another chapter of the law. He's been allowed to borrow a scroll from the prayer house. Holy Halfai is grooming Ishmael to sit at his feet and become an official apprentice of the law. I'm not happy about this, as it will mean he'll see more of Imma, who still hasn't forgiven me, even though she has no idea about what really happened. Ishmael has about as much talent for reading as my brother. My reading is much better but I bite my tongue except to praise. I'm trying to keep on Ishmael's good side and he hasn't hit me for a while. The text is written in the holy language, not the language we speak every day. I can more or less understand it, but I have to concentrate.

"This word here looks complicated," I say, pointing at the word *atonement*. I wait patiently as he mouths each syllable. When he eventually succeeds I whisper, "You'll have Holy Halfai sitting at your feet soon enough."

"You shouldn't call him that; it's not respectful," he says with a smile, and I feel as if I'm wobbling on the edge of an abyss, because for a moment he sounded like my father. I look down at the text, forcing my emotions to shut down. I don't even realize what Ishmael is reading aloud until a slow smile spreads over Rivka's face. Ishmael is so caught up in the memorization of each word that he hasn't realized either.

It's too much for Rivka to remain silent. "Ishmael, why don't you get Mariam to read aloud that last part a few times to help you really commit it to memory?" He nods, his brow furrowed as his lips silently echo each word.

I read, *"And the leper in whom the plague is, his clothes shall be rent, and his head bare, and he shall put a covering upon his upper lip, and shall cry, Unclean, unclean."*

"Do that last bit again, about the covering," says Ishmael, as Rivka smirks.

"Come on, Ishmael," says Rivka. "I expect Mariam memorized this bit ages ago."

I continue, *"All the days wherein the plague shall be in him he shall be defiled; he is unclean: he shall dwell alone; without the camp shall his habitation be."*

Ishmael manages to repeat this back to me without a single mistake and nods in quiet satisfaction at his success. Rivka looks satisfied too. I keep my face a blank mask. I won't let her hurt me.

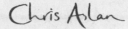

Instead, I imagine that I have the same terrible power as one of our prophets of old. "Be defiled forever," I declare dramatically in my head, and white, crusty bulges break out all over Rivka's face as she shrieks, falls to the ground, tearing at her hair and rending her garments, scraping at her face with shards of broken pottery. It almost makes me smile.

At sundown we eat together and I'm finally allowed to do all the chores that have built up over the day. It's late by the time I blow out the lamp. Rivka, Shoshanna, and Ishmael all appear to be asleep, but as I lie down next to him, I feel Ishmael's hands reach down the hem of my tunic, tugging it up. I never feel ready for his approaches, and try not to tense as it only makes his entrance into me feel more uncomfortable. He is like a farmer eager to sow his seed and digs deep in order to plant it. I hear him labouring on top of me, his mouth so close to my nose that I can smell the remnants of fish we ate for supper. I try to listen out for Rivka and Shoshanna's steady breathing, to reassure myself that they're still asleep. Then I try to think about something else. My mind wanders towards my brother, Eleazar, but thinking about him will only make me tense up more. Instead a memory surfaces from early childhood. I'd woken up in the middle of the night, thirsty for water. I could hear sighs and groans in the darkness, followed by a breathy chuckle. I didn't feel scared by the noises because whoever was making them sounded happy.

"Mother," I cried out. "Mother, I'm thirsty."

There was sudden silence and then the shuffle of clothing being adjusted, and I heard my mother's voice, a little strained, whisper, "Hush, Miri. Don't wake your brother and sister. I will fetch you water."

I felt her approach me in the darkness, patting me and then pressing a clay cup into my hands. I drank deeply and lay back, not quite satisfied because I knew that I had curtailed something secret and special.

39

Alabaster

***

Ishmael labours faster and then his whole body convulses, and with a strangled moan, he slumps on top of me. I'm relieved it's over. This is the only part I sort of enjoy, when he suddenly seems weak and vulnerable, as I bear his weight, and he doesn't bat my hand away if I caress the curls on the back of his head. It lasts just a moment before he withdraws, gets up and goes outside to cleanse himself. I'm about to follow him when I hear my mother-in-law whisper, "Let his seed settle in you and take root. You can cleanse yourself in the morning." Rivka lets out a loud, irritated sigh.

Grateful for the darkness, I lie there in silence and think about the many ways a person can be rendered unclean. Inevitably, my thoughts turn to Father.

I'd woken him in the night and we'd gone up to the flat roof. He'd seemed puzzled, but followed me silently. Then I lifted my lamp and asked him to remove his tunic. I held the lamp up against his back, close enough that he flinched from its heat. It was there: a pale white lesion with crusty edges and a leathery surface.

"Well?" Father asked quietly. I swallowed, unable to speak. "Miri?" Father turned and looked at my face and then he knew too.

"I would never have noticed it if I hadn't been wiping your back. No one needs to know. We don't have to tell anyone."

Father, his eyes shining with tears, was about to embrace me and then remembered and stopped. He paused in thought for a moment, his head bowed. "Yes, we could probably live like that for quite a while. The mark would grow bigger and possibly others would start, but for a while longer we could hide it." He glanced up. "Until one day it would be me raising my lamp and checking you or Marta or Eleazar and finding marks on you as well. Miri, this uncleanness will spread, not just over me but to others as well. How can I stay here and endanger you all, along with everyone else in our village?"

Chris Aslan

"I don't know. Maybe it's something else? We don't even know if it's..."

"I will present myself to Halfai tomorrow," said Father. "He will know."

We sat for a moment in silence. I tried to keep my voice steady. "Why is God punishing us? You were just trying to help that man."

Again Father reached for me and then stopped himself; a habit he would continue over the next few days with heartbreaking regularity. "Miri, I trust in him with all my heart, my mind and my strength. I don't understand this, but I'm not trusting in my understanding. I'm trusting in his."

I began to weep and Father watched, unable to take me in his arms. Then he, too, started to cry. I reached out for him. "No," he said, drawing back. "Please, Miri, you must keep your distance. Now go and wash your hands."

And that was the moment I began to understand the true evil of this disease.

It felt as if I didn't sleep at all that night until Marta shook me awake in the morning. "Where's Father?" I asked.

"He left without eating breakfast," she said. "He wouldn't say where he was going. Miri, is something wrong?"

I'm not very good at lying first thing in the morning, but was saved by the sound of one of our neighbours with three cows, who was walking the street with her milk pail, calling out for customers. Marta grabbed a jug and a few coppers and hurried outside.

I was still eating breakfast when Father returned, his face ashen.

"Marta," he said, standing back from us. "We have visitors."

Halfai, his wife Heras, and a gaggle of the village elders entered the compound, keeping as close to the door as possible. Marta quickly roused herself, bowing to the guests and hissing at me to fill a basin with water to wash their feet.

"No," said Halfai to her. "That will not be necessary. We are

41

not staying long." He looked around the compound. "Where is Eleazar?"

"I think he's playing with some of the other boys," said Marta. "Why? Has he done something wrong? Father, is Eleazar alright?"

"I can go and find him," I said.

"No," Halfai was abrupt. He turned to one of the elders who, with a silent nod, left in search of my brother. "You may not leave," Halfai said, turning back to us.

"I don't understand. Father?" Marta looked to Father but his head was bowed, his hair obscuring his face.

Clearing his throat, Halfai then announced, "This household is quarantined for seven days. For this duration you may not leave. At dawn, a water jug left outside your compound door will be filled with water. Likewise you may leave coins for any items you need to purchase. Heras will ensure that you have what you need."

"Quarantined?" said Marta. "Has someone died?"

Halfai ignored her and continued. "Marta and Mariam, daughters of Shimon, you will disrobe and present yourself to Heras for inspection. If there is any white spot upon you, it will be examined in seven days. If still present, you will become unclean to all others and you will be exiled from the village."

"Are you talking about leprosy?" Marta asked. "Why would we be at risk? I can't remember there being any lepers in our village for years."

Halfai and the elders prepared to leave. "No, you should stay here, Shimon," said Halfai to my father.

"But if my daughters must disrobe?"

"You may turn your face away until their examination is completed."

Marta and I glanced at each other and then at Heras. She was a plump, browbeaten woman who looked at us both with a blend of sympathy and wariness. She bolted the door after Halfai, and my father turned to stare at the trunk of the apricot tree.

Chris Aslan

"Must we disrobe here? Can't we at least go into the inner room?" asked Marta.

"The inspection must be done in sunlight. My husband knows about these things," said Heras. We began to undress, suddenly self-conscious, although we had bathed together many times. I tried to cover my breasts but Heras shook her head and mimed the position we were to take, with arms outstretched and legs apart. She began with Marta, running her eyes over every part of her body, but careful not to come too close or to touch us. "And now lift your heels, one at a time," she said. Then it was my turn.

I stared straight ahead, feeling goose pimples break out down my back, due to scrutiny, not cold.

"You may clothe yourselves," she said, once she was done. "You are both clean."

I glanced over at Father and saw his shoulders slump a little and his head tip back in a silent prayer of thanks.

As we slipped our tunics over our heads, we could hear Eleazar coming up our street. "Why do I have to come with you and the others don't? I haven't done anything wrong."

"Eleazar," Father called out, still facing away towards the tree. "That is no way to speak to an elder. Wait outside until honourable Halfai invites you to join us."

"Why? What's going on?" Eleazar whined.

"Eleazar!" Father shouted. I had rarely heard him raise his voice like this.

We dressed hurriedly, and once our headscarves were on, Heras went to the door, unbolted it and hurried out, clearly relieved to be leaving. Halfai entered, followed by a fuming Eleazar.

"Shimon, son of Hillel, and Eleazar, son of Shimon, you will disrobe and present yourselves before me," said Halfai formally. "Marta and Mariam, you will avert your gaze."

"What? I'm not – " Eleazar's voice was cut short by a look from Father. Marta and I turned to face the apricot tree as Father had done. "Will this do?" Marta asked. I glanced round and caught

43

a glimpse of Eleazar's face as anger was replaced with confusion and fear. We stared at the tree. My hands began to sweat and my chest tighten.

"Raise your arms like this, and spread your legs," said Halfai. After what seemed like an age, he said, "There is no mark upon you. You are clean."

Hearing this, I almost released my bladder in relief, but then a moment later he said, "Now you, Shimon," and I felt my stomach clench again. This time the examination took longer. I glanced at Marta. Her jaw was clenched. She wouldn't look at me, keeping her eyes fixed on the tree, just as she'd been told.

Halfai sighed. It was not a quick sigh of exasperation but slower and filled with sadness. "Shimon, son of Hillel, there is a white mark upon you."

I felt dizzy and wondered if I would pass out.

"It may be a temporary affliction. If it is gone within seven days, then you need only fulfil the purification rituals and return to your usual life. If, however, the spot remains, then you will be exiled from this village and may never return without warning those around you, declaring – for as long as you are able to do so – the words 'unclean, unclean'."

Marta gave a small cry and turned, forgetting that our father was still naked, and then quickly turned back again, struggling to breathe. We clung to one another, still facing the tree.

"You may robe yourselves," said Halfai, with a note of sympathy in his voice. "I will return in seven days."

We heard him leave and the door shut. "Fetch soap and fragrant spices. I must cleanse myself," I heard him say to his wife out on the street, and we heard their words of sympathy and pity grow distant as they walked away. Eleazar bolted the door. We turned around, and rushed to Father.

"No!" he cried, backing away. "You mustn't touch me. You can never touch me again."

Marta fell to the ground, dragging me with her, as Father

backed away towards the ladder leading up to the upper room and the roof. "I'm so sorry," he whispered hoarsely.

"I don't understand what just happened. Does this mean I have to stay here for a whole week?" asked Eleazar. For a moment I just stared at him, incredulous. Then I hit him as hard as I could across his face.

"Miri, please," Father sobbed, as Eleazar threw himself at me while Marta restrained him.

"I hate you!" Eleazar spat at me. "Why was I cursed with sisters?"

I wanted to hit Eleazar again and again and not stop. I saw Father step forward to separate us, and then step back when he remembered that he couldn't touch us.

"I'm sorry," I said, looking at Father and not Eleazar.

"This cannot be happening," said Marta, dazed, looking over at the carpet she had been working on a day ago when our world was still intact.

"Why can't it be you?" Eleazar hissed quietly at me.

"Please," said Father. "We cannot fight. Let's pray that this mark is just something temporary. God has shown mercy towards whole cities who turned to him. Marta, I will pray in the upper room. It's best I keep away from you all. Could you bring some bedding up?"

"But you can't sleep there. It's not finished," said Marta, ever practical.

"No, but it will have to do. It's only for a week," said Father.

"What if it isn't?" Marta asked. "If the spot is still there next week…"

"Not now," said Father, nodding towards Eleazar. "Miri, if you bring the bedding out and leave it here, I can carry it up the ladder."

"Wait," said Marta. "I'll sweep the room first and check for scorpions. We can also put a carpet down, and try to make it a bit more like home."

Father nodded. "I will be on the roof, praying," he said.

I was going to get the bedding but Marta put a light hand on my arm. "Please, let me," she said, because this was how Marta could show our father how much she loved him.

This meant that I was left in the compound with Eleazar. "You can't make me stay here," he spat.

"Do you think I want to be stuck here with you for a week?" I asked. "By all means, climb the tree and go swimming. How long will it be before Halfai sends his men after you? What do you think they'll do when they find you, eh?"

"I wish you had leprosy and had to be banished," Eleazar whispered.

I resisted the urge to punch him hard in the face. "What do I care about your wishes?" I said evenly. "Now go and study your letters."

Over the next seven days we each faced our quarantine more or less in isolation. Marta, who was happy to spend all day in the compound anyway, busied herself preparing Father's favourite dishes and working on her latest carpet whenever she had a spare moment. Father stayed praying in the upper room, coming down only to relieve himself. Eleazar, much to our surprise, sat in front of his wax tablet, his face furrowed in concentration, and learned more that week than in the past several months combined.

"Is there anything I can do?" I asked Marta, who just shook her head.

I went into the inner room and lay there in the dark, crying. By the time I awoke it was late afternoon. I was woken by the sound of breaking pottery. Wandering outside, I saw Marta smashing the shards from one of her favourite cooking pots with a rock from her herb border.

"What are you doing? That pot was Mother's," I said.

Marta was crying. "It's my fault," she said.

"What's your fault?" I asked. "Did you drop it?"

"No, it happened a week ago," said Marta. "It was raining and I'd left the pot outside to collect water. Then the next morning I saw that a gecko had drowned in it. I knew what I should do but I just fished the gecko out and poured the water away and scrubbed the pot clean."

She looked at my bafflement, and sighed in exasperation. "Miri, don't you know the law at all? The pot had been rendered unclean. I should have smashed it immediately but it was Mother's and one of my favourites…" Her voice trailed off. "Now God is punishing us," she whispered.

"You think leprosy is a fair punishment for a pot? What would God's punishment be for my cooking?" I asked, almost managing to make her smile. "This is no one's fault."

I heard what sounded like a stifled sob and looked up at the window frame in the upper room, but there was no one there.

That evening, while Marta had taken food up to Father, the first of our visitors came knocking. I went to the compound door and explained to whoever was there that we were quarantined and not allowed to let anyone in or out.

"I know," a voice hissed back. "The whole village knows."

"Aunt Shiphra!" I leaned against the door and we talked through the crack.

"How is your father?" she asked.

"I don't know. He just wants to be by himself and pray. I've been too busy keeping Eleazar out of trouble."

Shiphra gave a knowing laugh. "Yokkan seems to be missing his young shadow, with no one to impress. I've made a bowl of balm for your father. He needs to apply it morning and evening, after prayers. Here, I'll pass it over."

I looked up and the balm appeared over the mud-brick wall. "Thank you, Aunt Shiphra. Father will really appreciate this."

"And…" There was a short pause but long enough for me to notice. "There's no need to return the bowl."

"Thank you, that's very kind of you," I said, with a lump in my throat. "Give our greetings to Yokkan and Mara."

The next visitor was Imma. "I've been trying to find excuses to leave the house all day, but Mother's kept me busy. She knew I'd come straight here. I've brought water for you. I'll fill up the jar."

I hadn't realized that Marta had already placed a jar outside the compound as instructed. "What have your parents been saying?"

"Father is praying for your father now during the evening prayers. Mother wept when she told me the news and I've decided to start fasting from tomorrow. So have some of the other girls. Miri, don't lose heart. I know your father will get better."

I tried to speak but words wouldn't come.

"Miri, are you still there?"

"Yes," I sobbed. "Thank you, Imma. I don't know why I didn't even think of it. I'm going to fast too. Imma, what happens to Father if – "

"Don't think like that," said Imma. "God willing, everything will be alright. Everyone in the village loves your father. I'm sure God will heal him."

"Thank you, thank you so much, Imma." I wiped my nose on my sleeve.

"I saw Ishmael on my way here."

"Were his eyes on his sheep or on you?"

Imma laughed and then she told me the latest village gossip, determined to cheer me up. For the first time that day, even though I was talking to a door, I felt normal.

A little later there was another knock and a voice from outside. This time it was Annas for Marta.

"Come, Eleazar," I said. "We'll finish supper and leave Marta to talk in peace."

Eleazar's anger had fizzled on and off for most of the day but was now replaced with such a deep despondency that even I felt a bit sorry for him. If this had been a rest day he would at least have been able to go outside again now that it was past sundown.

Chris Aslan

"Is Father going to die?" he asked, as we sat down in the covered kitchen area.

"We're all going to die at some point," I said, not really sure how to answer him.

"But what if Father really is a leper?"

"He won't be. When I was chatting to Imma, she told me that everyone on our street is praying and fasting for him."

"But what if that doesn't work? What will happen to him?"

"It will work. If you want, you can fast as well."

"Are we all going to fast?"

"Except Father; he needs to stay strong."

Once Eleazar was in bed, and with Marta squatting by the door whispering to Annas, I went up to Father to collect his plate and cup and to give him the balm made by his sister.

"They're all praying for you and fasting; the whole village. The spot will go away, I know it."

Father sighed and rubbed his back against the unplastered mud-brick walls as if he could scrape away the spot. "Father, I've been thinking," I said. "And I have an idea." He looked up and I squatted down beside the ladder. "We could sell the jar. I could pass it on to Aunt Shiphra and then Cousin Yokkan could take it to the city. He could find a doctor there or a healer; someone who will come and make you better."

Father smiled sadly as I petered out. "Remember who gave me the jar, Miri? If a doctor could have cured him, don't you think *he* would have sold it? No, the jar is not for me. I've saved it for my children; for your dowries. Listen, if I'm not around – " I moved towards him instinctively but he shook his head. "Miri, I don't want you wasting the jar on some so-called doctor. There is no cure for leprosy. If that is what I have, then it's more important than ever that you keep the jar safe."

"Should I tell Marta?"

"Let's wait and see what this week brings," said Father.

"Father, what if – "

49

"Do you know why so few lepers come through our village?" Father interrupted. I didn't see why this was relevant. "You know it is our religious duty to give them food and alms, but the youths of the village, playing in the brook near the main road to the capital, they've always kept one eye on that road for undesirables. When I was not much older than Eleazar, three women came, in rags and with their bells, calling 'unclean, unclean' and begging. We threw stones at them. They cursed us but we didn't stop until we had driven them back towards the capital. That's what I did."

"But Father, you were just young and stupid like Eleazar."

Father almost smiled. "It's what I did, Miri. I cannot describe the shame I feel."

"Are you saying that you think God is punishing you? Because remember how you helped the man on our land – "

"No, I'm not saying that. If God wished punishment, he would have given the whole group of us leprosy." Father sighed. "What I'm trying to say is that if I saw those women now, I would give them the jar." He looked up. "That jar is your futures, Miri. You must take good care of it."

I nodded, picked up Father's plate and cup and carried them down the ladder.

"Don't forget to wash your hands afterwards," Father called out.

That night I waited until Marta and Eleazar were asleep, and then opened Mother's chest as quietly as I could. I removed the jar, wrapped it in a torn piece of burlap sacking, and in the light of the moon, dug a hole for it under the fig sapling Marta had recently planted, and buried it there.

Chapter Four

On the third day of every week, our village hosts a market. Makeshift stalls are set up around the well, joining the permanent ones, and the village teems with people. Although the capital can be reached in a day, people from smaller villages and settlements nearby prefer our market, as prices are cheaper. A few wholesale traders from the city come to buy olives, figs, and dates.

A month ago a new seller arrived. It was one of the first warm days of the year and she wore a tunic that barely covered her shoulders, with no robe. Although she wore a headscarf, it barely covered the braids brazenly visible beneath it. She set up a stall full of bright bolts of finely woven cloth, so different from our own homespun. The young men of the village developed a sudden interest in fabric, buzzing around her stall like flies on meat. As for the women, the wealthier clucked over each bolt of cloth, marvelling at the vibrant colours, while the poorer women tutted and shook their heads, bemoaning the corrupting influence of the West.

Despite these mutterings, the seller did brisk trade and returned the next week, even after Halfai denounced her during his holy day sermon. Now, respectable women lured to her fabric could only glance furtively from a distance before dispatching one of the loitering children to make the final purchase. Then, last week, Halfai, Ishmael and some of the other more religious men waited for her at the main road. As her heavily laden donkey came into view, they threw stones at her until she returned to the city. "Learn your lesson!" they shouted after her, Ishmael told me.

Today is market day and although I'm not particularly late fetching water from the well, the market is already in full swing; everyone wants to finish their trading before it gets too hot. I wait my turn and have just finished filling my water jar when I hear a flurry of exclamations and turn around. Around ten horses are trotting up towards us. Riding them are Western soldiers. They glance down at us in disdain. I notice that riding with her arms clasped shamelessly around one of the soldiers, is the seller. She hasn't brought any cloth with her.

The horses trot around the well until they've encircled it. "We now collect tax," says a soldier, speaking our language badly.

There are indignant comments from some of the stallholders, and cries of, "Our tax has already been paid" and "Someone fetch Halfai". I don't know what to do, as I'm hemmed in. Those on the periphery of the square melt into the shadows, wary yet curious. The soldier who rode in first stands watching as the other soldiers dismount and begin to collect all the takings from each stall. They don't count; coins just get thrown into cloth bags which are soon heavy. No one says anything or puts up resistance. We're not stupid. The only one to stay mounted is the female trader, who surveys the scene.

"He's not here," she says to herself. Then she says loudly, "Learn your lesson. Tell that to your holy man."

The soldiers begin to mount and I think it's all over, but then the one who speaks a little of our language points at me. "You," he says. "Drink."

I look down at my water jar, flustered. It's too heavy for me

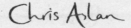

to pour slowly without water going everywhere, and if this idol worshipper drinks from it, then the jar will be unclean and I'll have to smash it. The soldier gives a nasty smile and points at the wooden bucket. I send it down and draw water for him. He comes over and drinks deeply from it.

"Again, for my friends," he says. The bucket is still almost full. He knocks the bucket into the well and I hear it ricocheting against the sides before it splashes down. He makes me draw a fresh bucket for each soldier. The rest of the village watches, aghast. For the first time in my life I'm grateful to Rivka, as she's given me plenty of practice in masking my emotions. The soldier clearly understands enough of our culture to know that each soldier is ritually polluting our only source of drinking water. We are learning our lesson.

When the last of them has finished, I put the bucket down. I'm sweating and it has the sour smell that comes from fear. I straighten my back and I think they're about to go, but then the same soldier looks at his friends and smirks. Then, in front of me, in front of us all, he urinates into the well. He's uncircumcised. He finishes and then looks up at me innocently, holding out his hands and gesturing for me to pour water on them. I pour the last of the water out. He flicks the water off, derisively, and then mounts his horse and, kicking up dust, they gallop out of the village.

"It's not your fault," says a woman behind me, putting a hand on my shoulder. I nod. I'm shaking.

"Where is Halfai?" someone shouts.

One of the village ladies selling dried figs is wailing. Judging by her empty baskets, she sold a lot today and now her earnings are gone. There are several women waiting with water jars who look at each other, shrug helplessly, and wander back to their compounds. I look down at my full jar and consider myself rather fortunate. When I get back, I tell Shoshanna what happened, and then she goes next door to fetch our neighbour, Ide, and I have to tell the story all over again. Even Rivka listens intently.

"This is Ishmael's fault," Rivka says at the end. "If he and Holy Halfai hadn't tried to stone a woman just for dressing well, we wouldn't be left drinking piss-water."

Shoshanna glowers. "Must you be so vulgar?" she asks, although she can't disagree. We begin a discussion about alternative sources of drinking water which is interrupted by a pounding at the compound door.

"Halfai wants everyone out by the well, even the women," a stout neighbour pants, before hurrying on to knock on the next door. Ide, overwhelmed by the sheer joy of this drama, is torn between going home to change her headscarf and the fear that she might miss something if she doesn't head to the well right now.

We trot down breathlessly together, Ide limping but just managing to keep up. I remember the last time the whole village turned out, but I manage to shake the thought from my head and look around. Ishmael and Young Shimon – not to be confused with Shimon my father – are dragging a chest from the sandal and saddle stall. Halfai directs them to place it beside the well and then he climbs on top, ensuring that despite his short stature everyone can see him.

"We are surrounded by enemies," he begins, without any formal introduction. "By Westerners and those seduced by them; occupiers of our land, enforcers of ungodly laws, corrupters of our youth; by whores who think they can come to our market under the pretence of selling something other than themselves."

Ishmael and Young Shimon clap and cheer him on, and soon the same villagers who were complaining a moment ago punctuate each statement with a cry of fury. Halfai raises his voice, spittle spraying upon Ishmael and Shimon like a blessing. "They dare to come here, on our own land, stealing from us, from our neighbours, our relatives!" I see one of the merchants who sells olive oil actually weep tears of rage and punch his fist in the air. "And what will we do about it?"

Someone shouts, "Holy war! We must rise up!"

This is greeted by excitement or alarm, depending on whether you're a stupid young man or a wiser woman. Halfai sees that he has whipped us up into a frenzy and is in danger of losing control. "I will tell you what we will do about it," he cries out. He pauses so that the crowd grows silent in anticipation. "Firstly, we will never forget. We will continue to support our young men who fight for our liberation and freedom. We will also take care of those who have been stolen from today. I call upon you all to give. Even the poorest of you must have a coin you can spare."

Young Shimon places a flat wicker bread basket in front of the chest, reaches into a pocket of his robe and pulls out three silver coins, dropping them ostentatiously into the basket. Ishmael does the same, and I glance over at Imma, who is nodding her approval. He is followed by Halfai, who ensures his gold coin flashes in the sun before he deposits it. I see stingy old Zechariah heading home saying he needs to fetch his coin, but we all know we won't be seeing him again today.

In our village, merchants are generally considered the richest and laziest, but who can refuse to come forward? The whole village is watching. Halfai calls representatives from each compound forward. I see Marta redden as her name is called, and she drops five copper coins into the tray. *What is she going to live on now?* I wonder, knowing she's nowhere near finishing her latest carpet, and needs every coin to feed herself. I glower at Halfai. My sister must pay for his stupid mistake. I will bring Marta food from our table tonight. I don't care if Ishmael beats me.

Finally, everyone has given. Halfai announces that the spring will be impure for seven days and that all drinking water must be collected from the sheep spring. That man has clearly never attempted to carry a water jar, much less scramble up the treacherous path frequented only by sheep. If this had happened in summer when the spring dries up, I don't know what we'd do. Halfai then announces that for the next seven days well water may be drawn for the purpose of watering our vegetable gardens. After that he will perform purification rituals over the well and the water will be fit to drink again. That's another problem with Halfai: he thinks everything can be sorted out with a seven-day delay.

For us, the seven days of quarantine merely allowed our lives to fall apart a little more slowly. Marta and I fasted for most of it. Nor were we alone. Each evening, Imma came and delivered well water and we talked together through the closed compound door. She'd try to encourage me by telling me of another villager who had joined in the fast for my father, or who was planning to give her dried fish or fresh figs to bring us, usually in cheap, hastily woven baskets which I soon learned not to offer to return.

When she asked me how Father was, and I would say, "He values your prayers, keep praying!", what I really meant was that Father had checked again that morning and the spot was still there and nothing had changed.

The food brought to us by the village robbed Marta of the distraction food preparation might have brought her. Anyway, only Father and Eleazar were eating, so we actually had more than we needed. Instead, Marta busied herself at her loom. I even joined her one afternoon, but after my sixth or seventh mistake, as she worried loose one of my knots in the wrong colour while sighing and blowing a strand of hair out of her eyes, I got the message and left her alone.

Eleazar also refused my help. He had taken to studying his letters with religious fervour and was determined to learn them by himself. When I asked what had motivated him, he looked up briefly and said, "I want to know the law. I want to know how to be clean."

I was left aimless. I prayed, although my mind wandered, partly due to hunger and partly because I wasn't sure who I was praying to, except that I repeated over and over again, "Let him be well, let him be well."

Chris Aslan

You'd think I would have cherished a whole seven days of Father's uninterrupted attention; that we would have sat together in the upper room talking and trying to keep each other's spirits up. Instead, the disease lodged a barrier between us which neither of us could breach even if we wanted to. Father constantly worried about us coming too close to him or touching something he had come in contact with. I felt guilty at how angry I was that he wasn't getting better – as if he somehow wasn't trying hard enough.

On the last night of the quarantine, Father removed his tunic and I peered at his back, holding the lamp as close as he'd allow me to get. There was no change.

"Miri, we need to talk," he said calmly.

"Father, there's still tonight. We're all praying for a miracle. Let's not waste our time making plans until we have to."

"That time has come," he said. "Perhaps the Lord will prevail at the last hour, but we must still make plans."

"Should I call Marta?"

He shook his head. "I want you to know that I'm sorry."

"Don't." I felt pain in my chest and my eyes blurred with tears.

"I should have been more careful with the man. I shouldn't have gone so close to him or touched him. I should have thought about my children and what it would be like for them to be orphans."

"Stop, Father; you don't need to do this."

"Do be patient with Eleazar. I know he can be difficult, but he needs you. Be strong for Marta. Let her care for you. She needs that. Use the jar to find yourselves loving husbands, and start new lives for yourselves. Promise me?"

I said nothing, and just nodded.

"And the jar. Is it safe?"

"I buried it."

"Good. I'm trying to remember the cleansing laws. They may have to break every pot in the house."

"Father..." I tried to swallow the lump in my throat. "I don't think we can do this. How can we cope without you?" Tears began to roll and Father made to embrace me and then stopped himself.

"I will visit," said Father. "As long as I stay outside the village and approach from the main road where I can be seen, I can visit. How could I ever be parted from you? I would die of a broken heart. How could I live without seeing you, the light of my eyes?" His voice broke with emotion. I sat, huddled. "Seeing you will keep me alive."

The next morning Father climbed down the ladder and informed us that the mark was still present. "Marta, I will need my travelling tunic, and a blanket and light sleeping mattress – nothing too big to carry – and some provisions." Marta nodded and wept silently as she prepared Father's request.

Then Halfai and Heras arrived with the elders. It was the same routine as the week before. Father and Eleazar faced the tree while Marta and I stripped. Heras supervised us and then examined us. She left and Halfai entered, and Eleazar and Father were next. Father didn't have to strip this time; he simply removed his tunic and stood there in his waist cloth. I was facing the apricot tree but heard the collective intake of breath and knew that Halfai and the elders had seen the white mark.

Once they were dressed again, Halfai opened the doors to our compound. A growing throng of villagers had collected outside and some of the boys were on the shoulders of their friends, staring over the mud-brick wall.

Halfai intoned the sentence, and Father tore his tunic as instructed. A basket spilling ash was placed on the ground before him and Father took a handful and scattered it over his head. A bell was placed in front of him with instructions to ring it wherever he went, to warn others of his presence, and he was instructed to tie a cloth over his mouth, lest his breath infect those around him.

"We will all accompany you as you make your final journey from our village," said Halfai. The crowd outside parted, careful to avoid touching the village leper, as Father stumbled outside.

"Keep your distance," shouted a voice at one of the youngsters who jostled too close to Father. The women from our street began to wail and keen as if Father was dead. A group of youths pushed their way through the crowd. They were Eleazar's friends, faces tear-stained. Eleazar froze for a moment, staring back at them. Then he turned and sprinted in the opposite direction, up towards the olive groves. The elders looked at Halfai questioningly, but he simply shook his head as if to say, "Let the boy go."

As Father watched his son abandon him, his face scrunched up and then he began to wail, beating his chest with his fist.

Marta and I dropped the sack we had prepared for Father to take into exile, and ran to him, but hands held us back.

"Let go!" Marta cried. I heard someone shrieking and then realized that it was me. I was being held by Elisheba, a woman from the other side of the village who had been friends with Mother. I tried to elbow her, but she drew me into a vice-like embrace, weeping but whispering soothing noises in my ear as Father began to walk forward.

Friends of Father walked behind him, weeping, and throwing ash over their heads and tearing at their tunics. Most of them were wearing their best tunics, and this honour they showed my father hurt like the twist of a knife. For a moment, I saw Auntie Shiphra and Marta clinging to each other, buoyed up by our neighbours, all of them keening and throwing ash over themselves and slapping their faces, and then with the jostling they were lost from view.

The whole village followed Father to the well and then out of the village, past the brook to the main road that led to the capital. Halfai was weeping as he laid a large pouch of coins on the ground before Father. "This is a collection from all of us. I wish I could embrace you. You will be missed," he said. I could see only the back of Father's shoulders, which were shaking. "The colony is two days' walk south. Follow the dried riverbed."

"Let me through!" I screamed. "Let me through!" Elisheba released me and I pushed forward. "I'm going with him," I declared wildly, wiping away snot with the back of my hand. "You can't stop me. He needs someone to take care of him."

"Please, don't do this," Father whispered, backing away.

"I don't care about the disease. I would rather die with you," I said, stepping forward.

"No," Father stumbled back, looking at me pleadingly. "Miri, don't do this. Don't make me throw stones at my own daughter. I will if I have to."

"Please, Father," I sobbed. "Let me come with you. Don't leave me here." Elisheba came up behind me and took me in her arms.

"I have her, Shimon," Elisheba called out.

"Please, take care of my children," Father said, addressing the village.

I heard Marta begin to scream. I had never heard her raise her voice like that before. Elisheba loosened her grip and I pushed through the crowd to her. We clung to one another, weeping and shrieking as Father turned, hoisted a bulging cloth sack onto his back, and trudged off alone into the wilderness.

Heras and the other elder wives waited patiently as Marta and I huddled sobbing beside the road as the rest of the village returned to their usual activities. Two of the women left and returned later with our donkey (which Halfai had minded during our quarantine) and three other donkeys, all laden with bundles.

"Come," said Heras, gently but firmly. "It's time for the cleansing."

We were led, numb and stumbling, down to the brook. Eleazar was already there with Cousin Yokkan and another of his friends who held up a sheet to screen him from us. We could see Eleazar's freshly shaven head above the sheet and the silhouette of Halfai flicking something at him. Eleazar then walked down to the water and bathed behind the sheet.

We waited as he scrubbed alone and had dressed in a new tunic behind the sheet, and then he was led off. One of the elder women stationed herself near the path to keep men away. The others, including Imma, unloaded the donkeys and began unwrapping cloth bundles of carpets, bedding, tunics, robes and headscarves. These were all tipped into the brook, letting the current wash through them before they were to be tackled with soap.

"Whatever we found in the upper room where your father stayed has been burnt," said one of the women. That included one of Mother's best carpets. Heras pulled out a sharpening stone and a set of shears and began sharpening them, telling us to strip as two women shielded us with the sheet. Everything we wore was thrown into the brook.

Marta's beautiful curls soon lay in heaps on the ground, ruffled by the evening breeze. Mine followed. Heras took out a sharp knife and a bowl of heated water and began to shave our eyebrows and then all of our body hair, finishing by shaving our scalps.

The absence of eyebrows left us expressionless, which probably mirrored the numbness we felt. We were both shivering from cold, exhaustion, and lack of food. Suddenly Marta's body was splattered with blood and then mine was too. It was still warm.

Heras continued to flick us with blood from a small bowl with a sprig of hyssop wrapped with scarlet wool, whispering prayers over us as she did so. I hadn't noticed the two doves. One had just been beheaded, the other struggled in Imma's hands. When Heras had finished with us, she also flicked the live dove with blood.

"Pass it to the girls," she said, and the bird tried to beat her wings against us. "Now, release the bird to freedom."

We let go of the dove and it flew off.

"Now bathe," said Heras, and gave us both a piece of spiced soap.

We scrubbed ourselves and it did feel good to be clean, even though by now our teeth were chattering.

"These new tunics are a gift," said Heras softly, as we emerged from the water. "And there are also new headscarves. They will hide your baldness and your shame."

Our clothes and bedding were still being washed as we were escorted back into the village. "Your home is being cleansed," Heras explained as she led us to Aunt Shiphra's compound. Inside, Mara – Yokkan's older sister – squatted over a pot by the hearth preparing lentil stew and puffing flatbread on a hot stone nestled in the embers.

We refused to eat but Mara insisted we try a ladleful each. The soup warmed through my body, and in the end I ate two bowlfuls.

After we finished, Auntie Shiphra, still red-eyed from weeping, pulled us to her ample frame. She rocked us for a few moments and then led us into the inner room. Eleazar was already asleep, his back to us. I lay down, and within moments I fell into an exhausted sleep.

Chapter Five

If I make it to the spring in one piece, it will be a miracle. This rocky sheep path was a challenging climb before, but after six days of constant use – with women skidding and slipping in the mud and spilling their jars – it is truly treacherous. I hold my empty jar with my right hand, nestled into the crook of my right shoulder, leaving my left hand free to balance or grab on to boulders. The thyme and mint which grows along the path sides is doing well with all this extra watering, and the path is too populated by women for any sheep to graze it. At my feet are the shattered pieces from a jar that was dropped.

I stop to let some other women pass with their jars full. They place their free hands in mine as I help them down this steep part. This makes me feel happy, because right now they are only focused on getting home without breaking anything and think nothing of touching a leper's daughter.

The spring itself is heaving with women. Some wait impatiently, staring angrily at the trickle which takes so long to fill just one jar. Others have settled themselves on the large rocks around, leaving their jars in a queue beside the spring. I put my jar at the end of the line. Elisheba, the older woman who was kind to me on the day my father was banished, is sitting with some of her neighbours, and beckons me over.

"Come, sit with us," she says. I notice a nervous exchange between two of the neighbours, who shuffle up the rock, allowing me more space than I actually need. These older ladies can sit with their legs sprawled in whatever position feels most comfortable, but I am careful to sit with my legs together. "And all this fuss because your husband and the other zealots didn't like the way a woman dressed," she says with a rueful chuckle. I redden and keep my gaze lowered. "Of course, I'm not blaming you, child. Look, men are like merchants, buying up rules as if they had all the money in the world, then it's we women who are the camels and have to carry the load for them." The neighbours chuckled.

The women talk easily with each other, occasionally pointing with their chins at the queue of jars. As the youngest I move our jars forward. I don't say much, but it feels so good to be included. Conversation inevitably moves towards matchmaking.

"He's a hard-working boy, even if he's a little on the short side," the first neighbour says, referring to her nephew. "And he has a thing for your sister-in-law," she adds, nodding at me.

"Rivka?"

"How many sisters-in-law do you have?" says Elisheba, and the others laugh. "Well?" she says. "You live with her. What do you think? She's always seemed a little stuck-up to me."

"My sister-in-law has been bred for royalty," I say, with a shy smirk. "She is never troubled with domestic duties and is merely required to wait until the king hears word of her."

The women slap their thighs and cackle. I can't help grinning myself. Usually I'd be careful with a comment like this – you never know when it will come back and bite you – but in the easy presence of these women, I forget about caution for a moment.

"The 'princess', that's what we'll call her," says the aunt. "I'll tell that nephew of mine to start learning to cook and fetch water!"

I worry that I shouldn't have said anything, but then we're called because their jars have reached the front of the queue. "Please, let me fill them for you," I say, and they don't argue. I help hoist a brimming jar onto each shoulder.

"Sisters, you go on," says Elisheba. "I want to talk with Mariam."

The women scrutinize the slough that was once a path, sigh, and then pick their way down. We return to Elisheba's rock. "How long has it been now?" she asks.

I know she means since my father was exiled. "Around two years," I say.

"And Eleazar?"

"Please, Auntie Elisheba, I don't want to talk about my brother."

Elisheba nods sympathetically. "Hillel, my son-in-law, leaves tomorrow for the north. I'll get him to ask around and see if he can find out anything." I thank her and we're silent for a moment. I sense that there is more Elisheba wishes to say. "Mariam, one of Hillel's colleagues returned from the capital yesterday with news."

I hold my breath.

"It's probably better that you talk to him yourself. He said that the authorities have begun a new campaign against the nationalists, the militants, and the insurrectionists. He said..." She pauses and swallows, and then lowers her voice. "He said that they've nailed up prisoners all along the road leading into the northern gates of the city. He said that they've spared no one. Young and old were nailed, whatever their age."

She puts an arm around my shoulder. I say nothing.

"I can introduce you to him if you'd like to hear more," she says, and I shake my head.

"What good would it do?" I say. "And please don't mention this to Marta or Mara or Aunt Shiphra. It'll just make them worried and there's nothing we can do."

Elisheba nods. "About your father," she says. "Hillel says that everyone in the north is talking about the new doctor. There is no sickness he cannot cure, they say."

I'm about to ask more, but one of the women shouts at me. It's my turn at the spring. I thank Elisheba and turn my attentions to my water jar. I angle it under the trickle of water from the spring above, and as it slowly fills, I ask myself silently how I feel; sometimes it's the only way I'll know, as no one else asks. I feel numb. If Eleazar was nailed or not, what difference does it make? As far as I'm concerned, my brother is dead to me. It's just me and Marta left.

After Father's banishment, Eleazar spent more time at Auntie Shiphra's compound than at ours. His devotion to Yokkan had grown even more since Yokkan had beaten up the first boy to make a joke about Father, and the first boy who tried to stop Eleazar from swimming with them in the brook in case he polluted the water. Auntie Shiphra also shared some of the stigma, being a leper's sister. It was hardest, though, for Marta and me. So many people in the village had prayed and fasted for a miracle and we were a living and constant reminder that those prayers had failed. I even hated myself for it.

Marta rarely left the compound, pouring all her energies into carpet-weaving. Whenever I suggested that she come and help up at our land with the olives, she found some excuse or simply said that we needed the income from the carpets she wove. Annas stopped calling round.

Nothing was spoken because the engagement had never actually been formalized. I don't know whether it was his choice or pressure from his father, but either way, who wants to take a leper's daughter into their home? Marta refused to talk about it but sometimes I'd hear her get up in the night to go outside, and I knew it was to weep in privacy. I bumped into Annas on the street a few times on my way to the well or returning from the market.

The first time he opened his mouth as if about to ask after Marta, but then stopped, nodded awkwardly, and hurried off. After that, whenever we met we would both nod to each other but leave it at that.

Eleazar and Yokkan began to sit at the feet of Holy Halfai and to learn the law. Eleazar burnt with an insufferable new religious zeal, and during the times he was actually home, he would recite long sections of it to us. Marta would nod encouragingly, her hands busy with cooking, cleaning, or weaving.

He became increasingly obsessed with purity laws. Marta was told off one morning in winter for huddling under her woollen shawl. "Don't you know it's a sin to wear wool and linen together?" Eleazar demanded, quoting that passage about not mixing fibres. He was also hard on himself. One morning I caught him slicing a nub of soap with a change of clothes draped over his shoulder.

"What are you doing?" I asked.

He reddened a little. "I must purify myself," he said. "I'm going to the brook to bathe and to wash these sullied clothes."

"El, are you mad? It's winter. You can't go swimming," I said.

"I'm not swimming. I'm washing. It is the law." Then clearing his throat and avoiding eye contact, he quoted the passage in the law that deals with semen emissions.

As he left, I looked at his broadening frame and realized that my little brother was growing up. I didn't like who he was growing into.

Soon the washing line was permanently hung with his drying waist cloths, and then he started enquiring about our menstrual cycles. "It's none of your business," I snapped.

"I am the man of this house," he replied. "And it is my duty to ensure that we keep our holy laws. If you and Marta are bleeding, then you shouldn't be sleeping in the inner room; you should go up on the roof, and wash your bedding afterwards."

"What an expert you've become," I glowered. "If you're so

concerned, then you can sleep on the roof. Or go and sleep with Yokkan. You spend all your waking hours together."

Eleazar stalked off and we didn't see him for over a week.

While Marta wove carpets and Eleazar studied the law and issued orders, I was left to manage our olive groves, to fetch water, and to go to market. At first I tried to drag Eleazar with me to the olive groves, knowing it wouldn't be appropriate for me to be alone up there as a woman. This precaution soon appeared unnecessary.

You see, there is something more contagious than leprosy that people fear catching through contact with the sufferer, and that's misfortune. Wherever I went I was accompanied by tongue clicks of pity, and whispers of "poor girl" and "shame", but never enquiries as to how I was doing, or even a hand on my shoulder. The girls with whom I used to joke and gossip so easily would now offer me their place while waiting at the well, and I would be offered cheaper prices at the stalls around the well. I learned to accept pity and distance.

Throughout this, Imma was the only girl who still talked and interacted with me as if I were a normal person. In fact, the first distancing of our closeness was not because of my father but because of Eleazar.

"I'm sick of him," I told her, as we sat under the shade of a large fig tree near the prayer house. "He and Yokkan do nothing but recite the law and tell us what we're doing wrong. Ever since they started sitting at the feet of – " I tailed off, realizing how insensitive I'd been.

"You mean, ever since they started sitting at my father's feet?" she said.

"I'm sorry; it's not your father's fault. He's our holy man. But these boys strutting around issuing orders…"

"I think it's good that Eleazar is studying under my father. He needs men in his life to show him the right way to live, and we need young men willing to fight for our nation."

Chris Aslan

"Yes, but you don't understand – "

"No, Miri, *you* don't understand," said Imma, and got up and left.

The hardest times during that first year of Father's exile, and the times I would long for, were when someone would come knocking at our compound door to let us know that lepers had been spotted out near the main road.

Marta would always press a few coins into my hand and tell me what to buy. I would run down to the market, make the purchases as quickly as possible, never haggling, and then head for the main road. Marta wasn't far behind, always keeping ready some of Father's favourite dishes, which she would wrap into fig-leaf parcels. Sometimes Aunt Shiphra and Mara would join us. Yokkan even joined us briefly once. Eleazar never did, managing somehow to absent himself every time. It just made me hate him.

Father was never alone. He explained on his first visit how lepers travel together, partly for protection from stone-throwers, but also because they lose the sensation of pain in their skin and rely on each other to spot injuries.

"Usually whoever's healthiest leads the way, which right now is me," Father explained during his first visit. He was squatting under a date palm while we kept the required seven paces from him, shielding our eyes with our hands from the glare of the sun. The other two lepers squatted further away from us in the scanty shade of another date palm, giving us a little privacy. One was once a handsome young man; now a lesion grew down his chin and the left side of his throat. The other was an older, stooped woman, in the advanced stages of the disease. "Auntie Demarchia has developed lesions on her eyelids, which means she scrapes her eyes every time she blinks, and now she's losing vision and needs me or Malchus to guide her," said Father. "She comes from a wealthy family in the capital and shares generously with us whatever they give her."

Alabaster

"What about the bag of coins the village gave you?" I asked. "Surely that will last you for a while."

Father smiled. "Don't be angry with me, girls," he said. "The colony is its own village; like a big family. The sickest people can no longer go out and beg, so we all agree to help each other."

"We're still your family," said Marta gently. "I'm glad you've helped others."

"It's really very interesting," Father continued, trying hard to stay positive. "We operate like a village but with different rules. It's acceptable, for example, for men and women who are unrelated to travel together. Rich and poor live together; leprosy makes us equal."

"How do you know all of this?" I asked. "You've only been there for a few weeks."

"My new friend, Gamaliel, runs our colony. Under his leadership, we've improved our tents and the permanent hovels. There's a better system for burying the dead and deciding who gets their bed. He's even planning on getting the colony some chickens."

"It sounds much better than I thought," I said. "And you look well?" I couldn't keep my voice from inflecting a question.

Father nodded. "The mark on my back is bigger, but it seems to grow slowly. Malchus washes it carefully for me each morning. I'm alive, and today I see my beautiful daughters! Just looking at you is nourishment for my soul."

"Father, when I do this," I said, hugging my arms around myself, "it means that I'm embracing you."

"And the same when I do it back to you," said Father, smiling, his eyes shining with tears. "And how is El?" he asked, trying to keep his tone bright and his eyes from leaking.

"Oh, you know El," I said. "He's always off playing with the other boys. He's become Yokkan's shadow and we don't see much more of him than you…" I tailed off.

"Well," Father coughed, and wiped his eyes. "I'm sure he's very busy. Tell him I love him and that I miss him."

Chris Aslan

"I'm sorry about El," I said.

Father shook his head. "Don't be hard on him, Miri. He's still young. He's just a boy."

We talked about general village news and passed on greetings from everyone.

"When will you come again?" Marta asked, after Father had called the other lepers over to eat with him.

"There is a system for everything in the colony," Father said. "No matter how much a village or town weeps and wails as it casts out its lepers, no matter how much they were loved or how high their social standing, no community wants to be visited by lepers. The most they can tolerate is about once a month. If I come more often, then instead of running to fetch you, the village boys will run to collect stones."

"But Father, you're one of us. You're from the village," I said.

"Trust me, Miri, it's always the same. I've learned a lot from Gamaliel."

And so, every month, Father would return. I soon sensed that he was right. Although friends of Father's and some of our distant relatives would press coins upon me when they saw me in the street, saying, "For the next time you see your father," no one outside our family ever came to see him.

Perhaps because we saw Father so infrequently, we were more aware than he was of the steady hold on him the disease took. I remember the first time he dropped a basket containing a large, baked red-belly fish from the Great Lake, a special delicacy. "It's alright," he'd laughed, peeling off the baked skin, now covered in sand, and blowing on it. "The insides are still nice and clean." His hands were becoming clawed.

"Mind, it's piping hot," said Marta, as Father tucked in anyway. I wondered if he was losing sensation in his mouth. Oil from the fish dribbled down his arms, and he rolled the sleeves of his robe up to prevent them getting stained, casually revealing another white lesion growing along the underside of his left forearm. We said nothing. What was there to say?

A month or so later, it was just Malchus and Father who came. "Please, Malchus, join us," said Marta. It seemed rude to leave him loitering alone. "How is Auntie Demarchia?"

Father and Malchus both looked worn out and tired. "She can't move any more and it's getting hard for her to breathe. It's inside her lungs now," said Malchus flatly.

"I'm so sorry," said Marta.

"Malchus, I remember how much you liked Marta's curds with date and pomegranate syrup," I said, trying to lighten the mood. "Here, there's enough for you to take back for Auntie Demarchia as well."

"Thank you," said Malchus, as he and Father picked without appetite at the large dried gourd-half Marta had filled. "But she's virtually stopped eating."

"That reminds me: I have more salve from Auntie Shiphra," said Marta, placing the wooden dish near them and then backing away.

"Please thank her for me," said Father. I noticed a roughness to his voice that hadn't been there before, as the leprosy worked its way inside him.

The next time Father and Malchus visited, Father was limping and leaning on a wooden staff. "I had an accident," he said, attempting a smile as Malchus helped him sit down under what we now referred to as Father's date palm. He stretched out his leg, which was covered in a huge welt. "I was trying to follow your recipe for lentil stew." He looked over at Marta. "And I must be getting clumsy because I managed to knock over the pot and was so busy trying to salvage the soup that I didn't realize how much had gone over my leg."

"Aunt Shiphra needs to see this," I said. "Let me fetch her. I'm sure she has a salve or a balm that would help."

Chris Aslan

"No, don't trouble her," Father rasped. He seemed to be finding it harder to speak. But I had already leapt to my feet and was running to Auntie Shiphra's house, grateful for the escape. Perhaps I wasn't so different from Eleazar.

"You just sit there, and drink some of this to calm you," said Auntie Shiphra, as I burst into the compound weeping. "Let me gather together what I need without you under my feet and then we'll go back and see your father together."

Father's leg recovered a little, thanks to the salves and balms Auntie Shiphra had concocted, but his body seemed to have forgotten how to heal properly. He still walked with a limp the next month we saw him. This time it seemed to take more effort for Father to speak and Marta, sensing this, asked Malchus to tell us more about his life.

"I was married, but God had yet to bless us with children," he said. "My wife was a beauty and all the men were jealous of me. I'm from one of the ten towns around the Great Lake. My father wanted me to follow him and my brother and be a fisherman. But I wanted a job where I could sleep at night and work during the day, and I saw how quickly the men would rush to get their catch sorted and to market before it spoiled. I saw an opportunity there and talked to one of the Western traders who told me how they smoke fish in his town to preserve it instead of salting it, which is expensive. So I started my own business. First thing in the morning I'd be on the shore waiting for the boats to come in with the night's catch, and by sundown whatever I'd purchased would be smoked and hung up to dry. It's not glamorous, but after a while you don't even notice the smell; not that I can smell much these days."

"And how long ago were you…" Marta tailed off, curiosity replaced with embarrassment.

"Cast out?" Malchus asked. "Around a year and a half ago my wife noticed the first spot. A week later, I joined the nearest colony. I wanted to stay close to my wife and to my father and brother. Then another man courted my wife and the holy man in our town declared that she was as good as widowed and gave them permission to marry. That's when I travelled down to the capital and then heard about the colony."

"I'm sorry," was all I could think of to say.

"It's hard not to let the changes on the outside change you on the inside, too." He took another slow mouthful. "I think we forgot to tell you last time. Auntie Demarchia is dead."

It was towards the end of summer when we saw Father for the last time. He and Malchus arrived together. The lesion on Malchus's chin had thickened and distorted his fine features even further. Father now had a lesion on his cheek, and his leg smelled as if it was rotting, although neither he nor Malchus seemed to notice. I wondered how ravished Father's body was under his ragged robe.

"Could El join us?" Father asked, once he and Malchus had assumed their position under the date palm and we had laid down platters of food and dried fish for them to eat. I looked to Marta, who seemed similarly uncomfortable.

"You know how he is, Father," she said. "Always running around somewhere. I could look for him, if you'd like."

Father shook his head. "He must be turning into a fine young man."

"I'm not sure about that," I said. "But he's the tallest out of the three of us now."

Father smiled. "I hoped I might see him one last time before I say goodbye."

There was a stunned silence as both Marta and I looked at each other, hoping we'd misheard. "What are you talking about?" said Marta.

Father sighed. "It's probably better that he remembers me as I was. No son wants to see their father looking like this."

"Father," I said insistently. "What's this talk of saying goodbye?"

"What's that?" For a moment, Father seemed to have forgotten where he was.

"There is no hope for us here," said Malchus. "Perhaps we'll live another few months or maybe a few years."

"Marta, there's a doctor in the north," said Father. "You must have heard of him. He's all people seem to talk about at the colony. They say he can cure any disease – even leprosy."

"We can still walk," said Malchus. "It's not too late for us. We want to make the journey north. Perhaps he'll see us. My relatives are there. They'll help us."

"Is this the same doctor old Cyria's been talking about?" I said. "She wants to take Crazy Mariam up to him. I heard her talking about it."

"Father, do you have any idea how long the journey will take?" said Marta. "Look how tired you are just walking from the colony to here. How will you possibly manage a long journey?"

"Hope, Marta," Father said gently. "Hope will strengthen us. Where else can we go? Where else is there hope?" Father's lip quivered and this sudden news of their departure took on a sense of reality.

"Father, there must be some other way," I said, my voice catching. "You can't just leave us."

"What is this?" Father rasped. "How is this life? We must always be seven paces apart. I am never to return any bowl or plate to you. I am trapped in this..." he batted at his chest with disgust, "...in this rotting flesh. I am a prisoner inside my own body. I am not a man, not a father; just a leper you pay to leave."

Father had always been so strong and so positive with us. This was the first time he let us see how he was really feeling.

"Wait," said Marta. "I'll fetch the donkey and provisions for your journey."

"No," said Father. "How will you collect the olive harvest? I

Alabaster

will not take anything more from you. I've taken your childhood; I won't take your future."

"Please don't go," I said. I didn't cry. I just felt a great emptiness stretch before me.

"The only thing that will break my heart more than leaving you is staying and letting you see me slowly decay," said Father. His voice cracked. "How I long to gather you into my arms right now."

I couldn't believe this was happening and that Father would actually leave.

Eventually, Father looked up. "The jar," he said. "Is it safe?"

Marta looked confused.

"Yes," I said. "Of course. I'll go and get it. It'll buy you a donkey with enough left over for everything you'll need for the journey."

"What?" said Marta.

"Marta, Miri will explain to you later," said Father. "No; this is not for me. It's my gift to you, my precious daughters. It will give you a future."

"We have no future without you," I said. "Can't we persuade you to stay?"

Father clambered to his feet, his face resolutely set. "Tell El that whatever he may think of me, I am proud of him. I am proud of my son. Almost as proud as I am of both of you. Look after each other. Have hope. Perhaps one day I'll return."

Malchus passed Father his staff. "I will still pray to our Lord for you every day," Father whispered, and with one lingering glance, he turned, leaning on Malchus, and they began to walk along the main road.

It might seem surprising, but neither of us wept. I don't think we really believed that we were seeing Father for the last time. We held on to each other as their silhouettes shimmered in the heat from the road. A caravan of camels approaching the village from the capital had to bypass them and we heard the high ringing of

76

their bells and cries of "unclean, unclean" above the clanging of camel bells.

We watched until we couldn't see them any more and the illusion that I had in my head that I could still pick up the hem of my tunic and run after them had faded. Still we stood there, not even shedding a tear. It was as if leprosy had infected us, working into our own hearts and robbing them of all sensation.

Chapter Six

The well is finally considered fit for drinking again. Life in the village resumes its normality. I'm behind with my chores after all the extra time spent fetching water from the sheep spring, so I arrive at the well late one morning. I've been feeling nauseous for the past few days, so I squat down for a moment, after filling my water jar.

"The heat getting to you?" a voice asks. I look up and see Cyria, mother of Crazy Mariam. I nod and she comes and sits on her haunches, unbidden, beside me. "My Mariam doesn't do well in the heat either," she says, and I wonder silently to myself if Crazy Mariam does well anywhere. "I've thought about tying a rope around her neck to stop her wandering off, but I'm worried she might choke. She's not an animal, either."

I turn to look at her. "How do you keep loving her?" I ask. It suddenly occurs to me how rude the question might sound, but Cyria doesn't take offence.

"She's my daughter," says Cyria which, I suppose, is answer enough. We squat in silence for a moment and then she asks, "Was there ever any news from the north about your father and that other leper?"

I shake my head.

"Don't give up hope. I always wanted to take my daughter to see him, but… I hear some of those gossips wondering what your father did to be cursed like that but I always butt in and tell them that he was a righteous man," she says.

I shade my eyes and turn to look her in the face. "Thank you," I say. "I haven't always done the same for you. I'm sorry."

"I understand. No one wants the attention on them, but that daughter of mine makes sure we're never forgotten, that's for sure. They should pay me for all the entertainment we give them."

I touch her shoulder for a moment and then heave myself up before offering her a hand. She lifts my water jar and places it in the crook of my shoulder. We nod to each other and then I return to the compound.

Shoshanna is slicing cucumber and mixing it with chopped mint and yogurt. She looks up briefly as I enter the compound, and then resumes her work. We're getting short of flour so I set myself up by the millstone with a bag of grain. I haven't been grinding for long before Rivka enters, slamming the compound door behind her.

"What's the matter?" Shoshanna asks.

"I've heard what you've been saying about me." Rivka storms over to me. "Princess, am I?"

I look up. "I don't know what you're talking about," I say. I am in such trouble.

"Don't lie," says Rivka. "You're lucky I'm not interested in him, otherwise I would have told them all about your dirty little secret."

I look to Shoshanna, who is clearly alarmed, hoping she can rescue the situation. "Mariam, what have you been saying?" she asks, coming over.

"Nothing," I say. "I made one little joke with some of the ladies at the spring."

"One little joke?" Shoshanna jabs each word with a sharp finger into my shoulder. "There is no such thing as one little joke.

Chris Aslan

You know that there is nothing more precious than a woman's reputation, and nothing more fragile. How could you spread lies about my daughter?"

"Mother, I will tell them all, I swear it," says Rivka. "They should take her outside the village and stone her, the whore."

"Rivka, please," says Shoshanna, trying to soothe her daughter. "Let me handle this." She wheels round on me and my heart thuds, because I know where this is leading. "Why was I cursed with a daughter-in-law like you? Do you think Ishmael will be happy to hear that you've been ruining his sister's reputation?"

What she means is that she will tell Ishmael tonight when he comes home tired and cranky, and then he will beat me everywhere but my face, which must remain unbruised in order for us to be a respectable household.

"I'm so sorry," I whisper, already feeling fear, the panic of the thought of the beating making it hard to breathe.

"Sorry?" Shoshanna looks at me in astonishment. "What use is 'sorry' when you tarnish my daughter's reputation? You're lucky I haven't thrown you out!"

"Please," I say. "I haven't bled yet."

Shoshanna looks ready to hit me but stills her hand.

"It's true. Look, I'll show you." I scurry into the inner room and bring out the cloth lined with rags that I usually tie between my legs during my monthly bleeding. Rivka and Shoshanna started bleeding two days ago.

Shoshanna looks at it, then bends down and sniffs me and nods. I can see her weighing up the punishment she thinks I deserve against the risk of losing a potential grandson. In the end she slaps me hard, once, across the face. "Rivka," she calls, and Rivka comes and does the same.

My head spins, and it hurts, but I've got off lightly. I resume my grinding and silently curse Elisheba's neighbours. This will not be easy to fix. How could I have been so stupid? Rivka's spite means that she might spill my secret even if it damages her family's

81

reputation. As I continue with my grinding, I silently curse the whole family. They have ruined me.

If I hadn't married Ishmael, perhaps I would have recovered. After all, although we were sadder after Father left, life also became a little more bearable. Both Marta and I felt a guilty sense of release. We missed him greatly and prayed each night for him to find the northern doctor, but were grateful not to have the monthly reminders of his deterioration. Almost imperceptibly, attitudes towards us changed. People no longer clicked their tongues in sympathy when I passed, or asked after my father. For them, he was dead, which was sad, but people die all the time; the village had moved on.

We tried to move on as well. Marta began a campaign to win Eleazar back to us. She cooked his favourite dishes, and regularly sent me round to Aunt Shiphra's to fetch him back for supper. Aunt Shiphra's help was also enlisted, with the result that Yokkan and Eleazar would join us for an evening meal one night and then go to Aunt Shiphra's the next.

Marta pandered to Eleazar's every legalism, making sure that our household fully complied with every religious law. She encouraged him to sit at Halfai's feet rather than helping me with the olive harvest, and even gave Halfai coins that we could scarcely afford to pay for his studies.

Eleazar grew more arrogant by the day. I generally kept quiet for Marta's sake. I knew that she needed someone to take care of. Still, my resentment for him grew. One night I had a dream that the fevers which had plagued him as a child returned and that he died. I woke up and realized that I felt nothing personally at the prospect of my brother's death, except sadness for Marta.

Imma was really my only friend and she tried to lift my spirits. I didn't see much of her, as her parents were strict about letting her out of the house except for chores. She often praised Eleazar and the progress he was making in studying the law. I was careful to nod and smile and to keep my opinions to myself. Imma was also becoming more religious, although she would still blush and giggle when I joked about Ishmael.

"I watch him when Mother's not looking, and he has this earnest look as he sits at Father's feet, as if he mustn't let a single word Father speaks be forgotten," she said, as we sat under a peach tree near the prayer house.

"I've seen the earnest look he gets when he thinks you're not looking, too," I said, and she pushed me, laughing.

"Does he really?" she asked, after a moment.

For the most part, though, I learned to relish my own company. During summer I would often go up to the olive grove with the donkey, coming back loaded with sticks and branches so we wouldn't have to waste money buying firewood for cooking. It wasn't appropriate for me to be up there alone, and no doubt some of our neighbours tutted, thinking that this was what happened when a daughter was left with no father to guard her honour. Still, there was no other choice, and I kept out of other people's way.

Summer finished and the olive season began. I would leave the compound at dawn, taking food to eat along the way, and head up to our grove. I was determined to harvest our olives singlehandedly, to prove that a woman could do it. The first time I passed Annas he offered to help me, but I didn't want his help or his company. If he felt guilty for abandoning my sister, I wasn't going to help him salve his conscience.

One evening, as I led the donkey back down the path, saddlebags bulging with fresh green olives, Ishmael approached from a different path, throwing rocks at any of his sheep who dawdled to nibble on scrub. We nodded to one another.

"It's getting hard to find good pasturage for them," he said, as we trudged down together towards the village. "What's the grass like up in your grove?"

"It's all dried out, but there's enough to keep the donkey busy. Have you tried up along the ravine?"

"Should I?" he asked. There was something a little too direct about the way he was looking at me. "Well," he said as we neared the village. "You can go first and I'll follow in a little while, so it doesn't look like something."

"So what doesn't look like something?" I asked, irritated that he was making more of our conversation than just politeness. I could see that my tone upset him, so I added, "Look, Ishmael, I'm a leper's daughter. I've stopped worrying too much about what people think of me."

The next morning I had already started beating my first tree when the clanking of sheep bells alerted me to Ishmael's presence.

"Heading up to the ravine?" I asked.

"You're not going to try to harvest all these trees by yourself?" he said.

"Why not?" I replied. "And anyway, who else is going to help me?"

"What about Eleazar?"

"He's too busy sitting at the feet of Holy Halfai."

"I could help you."

"You've got your sheep to think about."

"We could do a deal: you let my sheep graze in your grove and I'll help you with your olives."

I blew a strand of hair out of my eyes and thought for a moment. "You can start with the tall tree over there. I'm guessing you're a good climber." I pointed at one of the trees further away. Ishmael ignored the tree I pointed to, shrugged off his robe and quickly clambered up the gnarled trunk next to me in his waist cloth, not tucking it between his legs as modesty would dictate. He began beating the branches vigorously, accompanied by the patter of falling olives.

We beat in silence. I could feel his eyes on me, and if I glanced up, he'd grin and hold my gaze as I quickly looked away. The day grew hotter, the beating and pattering blending with the whir of cicadas and the clanking of sheep bells as the herd ambled around us. Ishmael finished harvesting his first tree and swung down.

"Do you have a sack for me?" he asked.

I fetched the least stained one to give him. He brushed my hand in a way that didn't feel entirely accidental as I passed it to him.

We continued harvesting until noon. I noticed with annoyance and gratitude that he'd managed to harvest almost twice as much as me. If I was honest with myself, I was also enjoying his company and his attention, which made a pleasant change from the pity I was accustomed to from others.

I needed to relieve myself, and made sure I walked a good distance away before squatting behind an olive tree. When I came back, Ishmael was stretched out in the shade of one of the trees, resting.

"What?" he said, as I averted my eyes from his splayed legs. "We must have earned a break by now."

I passed him a leather water-skin and he poured it, gulping and swallowing with his mouth open, the way all the boys in our village learn. "I would have prepared more food if I'd known you'd be helping," I said, laying out my cheese, bread, and cucumber on a small cloth.

"I've got my own midday meal," he said, getting up to fetch it. He tossed a bundle of bread and sheep cheese at me, nodding with mock admiration as I caught it. I couldn't help but smile.

"So, you don't actually hate me," he said.

"I never said that I did."

He grinned and came back to the cloth, sitting nearer to me this time. "Good," he said, leaning close to me.

"Shouldn't you put on your robe?" I said.

He shrugged. "It's hot."

"Well, at least fold your waist cloth properly – you're gaping."

"Oh, so you noticed," he said, making no attempt to fold it. I knew that I should be careful. I could hear the voice of my mother in my head. "Mariam, my girl, what is more important to a woman than even a husband or sons? It is your reputation. Nothing is more precious or more fragile."

"What are you thinking about?"

I was quiet for a moment. "I'm thinking that after midday meal, you should probably take your sheep elsewhere."

"After midday meal," he said. I said nothing and we ate in silence. My hands trembled, which irritated me, particularly because he seemed to notice everything. I felt a lightness in my stomach and couldn't decide if it was a good feeling or a bad one.

"We've got time for a short nap after all that hard work," he said after midday meal, laying down his robe and then stretching himself out on top of it.

I sighed in exasperation. "Don't play with me, Ishmael," I said. "It's time for you to leave."

"Here, give me a hand up," he said. I gave him my hand and he yanked it, toppling me over.

"Let go of me," I said, flailing around on top of him. He just laughed as if we were playing, but at the same time he pulled at his waist cloth, loosening it.

"Come on, just a quick nap," he said, and managed to roll me over so that he was now on top of me, holding me between his legs. His waist cloth had come off.

"Seriously, Ishmael, just stop it," I snapped, trying to crawl backwards.

"You stop it," he breathed, pinning my arms back above my head and then reaching down to pull up my tunic.

"Argh! Please, just let me go."

Instead, he pressed his mouth onto mine. I struggled but he was stronger. I tried to pull my tunic back down and then gasped as he pushed something hard inside me.

"Please stop," I whimpered. But he didn't. Stones jutted into my back and I looked around wildly to see if there was one I could grab and hit him with. Instead he loomed over me, his hair forming a tent around my face, locking me in.

"Stop," I groaned, and kept on saying it until, finally, he did.

He collapsed on top of me. For a moment I thought he might

be dead. His hands relaxed their grip on my wrists and his forehead rested on mine. Then he pulled himself off, suddenly modest, and turned his back on me while he wiped himself with his waistcloth. Now it was spotted with blood and something else. I pulled my tunic down, even if it was too late, and curled myself away from him, sobbing into my headscarf.

"Oh, come on," I heard him say, with a sigh of irritation. "Don't tell me you didn't want it." I continued to weep. "Look, no one needs to know about this. I won't tell anyone and I know you won't."

I carried on weeping and then heard him swear and start rounding up his sheep. I kept my head buried in my headscarf as if I could actually hide inside it, waiting for the clank of bells to diminish. Still, I just lay there, curled up. I didn't know what else to do.

Eventually, I managed to sit up. Everything hurt down there, inside. I got to my feet and adjusted my tunic. I don't know how the next few hours passed; I honestly can't remember. What I do know is that before I went home, I bathed in the brook, washing my tunic and my headscarf, and then walked the donkey the long way around the village so that no one would ask me why I was wearing damp clothes.

At home, Eleazar was mercifully absent. Marta looked up briefly from the pot of lentil stew she was stirring. "Are those clothes wet?" she said.

"Don't worry. I'll change out of them now," I said.

Later that evening, Marta chided me gently for walking home in wet clothes, assuming that they were the reason I was feeling ill and not talking at all at supper, just wanting to go to bed.

The next morning, I passed several people on my way up to the olive groves. I waited for them to stare at me in shock or in horror. Couldn't they see that I was broken?

"A woman's honour is like the wings of a butterfly," was another of Mother's sayings. "Beautiful yet fragile, and without them she is but a worm."

Couldn't everyone see that my wings had been ripped off?

I didn't tell anyone. I struggled on with the harvest, but froze every time I thought I heard the clang of a sheep bell. I left later and returned earlier. Each day my sack of harvested olives was lighter. I felt hollowed out, as if something had pecked away at my heart and my spirit until there was nothing left but a wretched, lonely numbness.

Ishmael passed me a few days later. He grinned and it sickened me. When he saw my expression, his own became hard as well, and he simply continued as if he hadn't seen me, throwing stones at his flock to keep them moving.

The next time I saw Imma, she barely asked me how I was before making a joke about how she envied Ishmael's long eyelashes, so wasted on a man.

"Don't talk to me about him," I said, and walked away leaving her perplexed.

My sister could sense that something wasn't right. Although I determined to forget what had happened, I'd still wake up shaking, with Marta wiping my damp forehead and whispering comfort.

Then came the time when Marta laid out rags for us to use during our monthly bleeding. I didn't bleed. For a few days I convinced myself that it was just late and strapped the rags to me anyway. I started to feel nauseous in the mornings and Marta reluctantly joined me up in the grove, harvesting olives. My breasts felt sore, I needed to urinate more often, and still no blood. Finally I picked an evening when we were alone and told Marta what had happened. She listened without interruption, holding my hands. When I had finished, she embraced me and then rocked me gently, whispering, "My poor, poor Miri."

It was such a release to tell someone, even though the problem remained. "I must go to Aunt Shiphra," she said. "We need help."

I didn't want anyone else to know, but I knew she was right, and my protest was half-hearted. When they returned, Aunt Shiphra

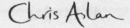

Chris Aslan

had already been given the general gist. "Come here, my peach."
She hugged me fiercely, and then felt my belly and prodded my
breasts, standing back to look at me. "You can't tell yet. You're
young and you favour baggy tunics," she said. "At least we have a
little time."

Then she made me go over the story again, quizzing me over
every shameful detail. "Well, you clearly did not consent and this
is a case of rape. Ishmael could be stoned for this."

"Good," I said.

"Not really," she sighed wearily. "The news will spread and
the whole village will be dishonoured. His family will protest and
say that you encouraged him or even seduced him, so there will
always be doubt cast upon your honour. They might even sway
popular opinion enough to have you cast out or stoned. If you
think being a leper's daughter is bad, this will be worse."

"What can we do?" said Marta.

Aunt Shiphra rocked on her haunches, thinking. "Let me speak
with Shoshanna," she said, finally. "Perhaps there is a way to work
this out."

"How can this ever work out? He raped me. He put this curse
inside me."

"Hush, Miri; that's no way to speak of the blessing of new
birth," said Shiphra. "You wait here. I'll go and see her now."

She left, and returned quicker than we had expected. Shoshanna,
wide-eyed and anxious, was with her.

"I thought it would be better that we talk here, in private," said
Shiphra.

"And what of these girls?" Shoshanna pointed at us.

"This girl is why I asked you here," Shiphra nodded at me.
"Your son raped her." Shoshanna listened in shocked silence as
Shiphra told her what had happened.

"This cannot be true," Shoshanna said finally. "My son is a
religious man. He would never do such a thing. The girl is lying."

"I swear on the life of my sister that it is true," I said.

Shoshanna tutted dismissively. "A girl who loses her reputation will swear by anything."

"She will swear before Halfai and before the elders," said Shiphra slowly. This elicited a quiet gasp from Shoshanna.

"That is a dangerous move to make; they could both be taken out and stoned," she countered.

"A woman who has been robbed of her honour has nothing left to risk."

"I must talk with my son, and hear what he has to say."

She left and we waited. Marta boiled water for mint tea.

"She didn't scream," said Shoshanna triumphantly, striding back in.

"Who would have heard me?" I said. "We were alone in the olive grove."

"And why were you alone? Surely you knew what people would say? You seduced my son. Come on, admit it."

"I told him to stop. I fought him. It was rape."

"No. You told him that you had already lost your reputation, as a leper's daughter. What more invitation does a man need?"

"You twist my words!" I shouted. "I will go to Halfai right now and see Ishmael stoned." I looked to Aunt Shiphra and Marta for support. Aunt Shiphra gently shook her head.

"Sit down, Shoshanna," said Shiphra curtly, nodding towards the place of least honour nearest the compound door. "Let's get down to business."

As they haggled over the bride price and the bridal contract, I wandered over to Marta, unnoticed.

"Say nothing about the jar," I whispered. I had told her of it after Father had left. She glanced at Mother's chest, where we now stored it. "After all, he's taken enough from me already."

Finally it was agreed that they would pay for the wedding celebrations, but that we would contribute our one remaining sheep that had been a lamb when Father sold the others. Ishmael

was already shepherding it for us, so that part was easy. Aunt Shiphra drove Shoshanna hard when it came to the dowry.

"You must provide the dowry – all of it," she said emphatically.

"But this is not the custom. People will talk," said Shoshanna. "They might suspect something."

"Then buy it in secret. You will include a chest, a gold nose-ring – and don't think you can cheat me when it comes to gold – seven new tunics, a new robe, and two new headscarves, a bridal sheet, and the usual number of new mattresses and bedding for a married couple."

"But we aren't prepared! I have my daughter's dowry to save for."

"Maybe the son you raised should have thought about that before he raped my niece," was Shiphra's testy reply.

I almost smiled. Aunt Shiphra was good, and Marta had been right to ask for her help. Even Aunt Shiphra accepted that we must pay the bride price ourselves. It was supposed to be fifty large silver coins but, after further haggling, became ownership of the other two remaining sheep in their care, which would belong to Ishmael if he ever divorced me.

Aunt Shiphra, as a woman, couldn't legally represent me, so it fell to Father's cousin, Yoezer, to speak to Halfai with Ishmael and have the marriage contract drawn up. I heard from Uncle Yoezer what a pious man Ishmael was and how he'd told Halfai that this was an act of charity, bestowing mercy on a leper's daughter. It was a clever move by Ishmael to gain Halfai's approval, given that Halfai himself must have known that somewhere else in his compound, his own daughter sobbed, heartbroken.

Imma only spoke to me once after the contract had been signed. "I will never forgive you for this theft," she hissed quietly, making sure no one else was listening. "You are dead to me, Mariam, dead."

I longed to explain what had happened and to tell her of her own lucky escape, but how could I? Her father could have me stoned, and who would believe the testimony of a girl?

91

It was left to Marta and Cousin Mara to hold up my side of the wedding canopy on the day Ishmael and his friends came for me. Ishmael, to my further amazement and disgust, entered into the spirit of the wedding, enjoying being the centre of attention instead of burning with shame. I was grateful for the full veil that hid my tear-stained face from the curious stares of others and meant that no one could see my expression whenever I was told what a charitable husband God had provided.

During the week leading up to the wedding, Shoshanna had made sure that everyone knew that she supported the religious zeal of her son and this act of piety, and made a great show of welcoming me as her new daughter into their compound. My dowry chest had been delivered two nights before, waking Marta up. It contained seven tunics which we suspected were not new. We decided not to mention this slight to Aunt Shiphra, who came the following morning with a needle and a smoothed twig. She pushed the twig up one nostril and then pierced my nose with the heated needle, pushing the nose-ring through as Marta and Mara held on to my arms and I squirmed in agony.

My greatest worry was the wedding sheet which would be displayed the following day as proof of my virginity.

"Don't worry about that," Aunt Shiphra had said. "It's been taken care of."

Late that night, Ishmael led me into the inner room, which had been prepared for us, with the marital straw mattress in the centre of the floor, covered in the white linen wedding sheet. Ishmael tried to remove my veil but I wouldn't let him, even if he removed my tunic. When he entered me I still gasped in pain, but it wasn't as bad as the first time. I glanced over to the doorway, where Shoshanna was watching dutifully to ensure everything was done correctly. When Ishmael had finished and was still sprawled on top of me, he fumbled under the mattress and found a knife she had left there for him. Shifting me to the side, he drew it down his inner thigh and blood welled, then he lay on top of the sheet for a moment, allowing it to soak in. The door closed and we were left alone.

"See, I bled for you," he said, smiling as if this had made everything right. "We got away with it," he added, before yawning, rolling over, and falling asleep. I just lay as still as possible, filled with a desperate sense of hopelessness.

Chapter Seven

The last time I saw Eleazar and Yokkan was through the weave of my veil at my wedding. Marta called for me the following morning, just as Shoshanna was hanging up the stained wedding sheet for all to see. We climbed up onto the roof of the house, which had a low wall around it, giving us a little privacy. Marta was distraught.

I listened with disbelief that turned to rage as she explained that Eleazar and Yokkan had run away. My brother's selfishness was breathtaking. It seemed to be a special knack of his to abandon those who loved him most at their hour of greatest need. How was Marta supposed to live in the compound alone, without a man? What would people say? It would be a disreputable and lonely existence. I would never have agreed to the marriage, whatever the consequences, if I'd known Marta would be left without family. I cursed him loudly, but that just elicited a fresh bout of sobbing from Marta.

Who would finish harvesting the olives? None of them had been brined. Who would protect the honour of our compound? Of course, my brother – that dog – had given no thought to any of these questions, or if he had, they hadn't stopped his stupid fantasies of martyrdom and holy war. Furiously, I prayed under my breath that he would suffer a painful and premature death.

The only glimmer of good to emerge from this situation was that the village gossips now had something far more interesting to discuss than suspicion over a hastily arranged and poorly matched wedding. Shoshanna's neighbours, who came to help clear up the compound and the upper guest room, speculated whether the boys had joined the nationalists, the zealots, the fundamentalists, or the insurgents. These groups were all largely the same, fighting against Western rule, but no one doubted that holy war was their aim. Some of the neighbours blamed Halfai for radicalizing them, and others pinched my cheeks and congratulated me for being sister to a holy warrior.

Later that day, after the relatives and neighbours had left, Ishmael slept and the house was quiet. I went to put on my headscarf and one of my supposedly new tunics. "Where do you think you're going?" Shoshanna snapped.

"I have to go and see my sister and Aunt Shiphra," I said. "They must be devastated about the boys leaving."

"And you didn't think to request permission from me?" she asked.

In reality, I hadn't. I'd grown so used to my own freedom, it hadn't occurred to me that now that I was paid for, I was also owned.

"Sit. This is your family now," said Shoshanna.

"But – "

"I said sit!" she barked. So I sat. "Now listen to me, girl." She glanced at the closed door to the inner room where Ishmael slept. "This mess was not my making. I didn't choose this. I did not choose you. I don't know who was to blame for what went on up in the grove, but I do know that it wasn't me. You think I want someone like you living in my house, under my roof? You will do everything I say and if you don't, I will make sure my son beats you until you do. Do you understand?"

I nodded.

"Now, get out of my sight," she said, and I looked around the cramped compound and wondered where I was supposed to go. "No, make yourself useful," she added, pinching the bridge of her nose as if she had a headache. "Make some mint and sage tea."

Over the next few days, Ishmael looked for excuses to get his mother and sister out of the compound. Then he'd lead me into the inner room and he'd take me noisily and hungrily, often more than once. I felt ashamed every time, and asked him to keep the inner door closed.

"But then I won't be able to see what I'm doing," he grinned. I grew used to seeing him naked and aroused, but any desire for him I might have once felt had withered. Each time he approached me I could taste bile in my throat and felt sick to my stomach.

Most mornings began with me squatting over the hole in the unclean place, vomiting. This meant that Rivka was dispatched to fetch the water, something she clearly resented even more than my general presence in the compound. She knew the real reason Ishmael had married me, and had been sworn to secrecy about my pregnancy, which we would only announce a month after the wedding.

On days I was well, I collected water. I almost collided with Imma once. True to her word, she gazed through me as if I was invisible. I felt utterly alone. I started to think that the child growing inside me might not be such a bad thing after all. At least I would have someone to love.

Ishmael rarely paid me much attention except when he was on top of me. But sometimes, afterwards, he would rub my belly and speak to it.

"How's my boy?" he would whisper. "Will you be as strong and handsome as your father? When can I start teaching you how to use a sling?"

I wasn't happy, but life wasn't unbearable. My heart ached for Marta. She tried visiting once or twice, but Shoshanna made it clear that she was not welcome. We met occasionally at the well. Marta had aged dramatically. She'd lost weight and her skin looked grey and lifeless.

"I'm praying for Father and El," she said to me one evening, after we had embraced near the well. "They are both still alive. I can feel it in my body."

"I hope you're right," I said, thinking more of Father than Eleazar.

"I know it," she said, with a crazed certainty that just made me worry for her more.

I saw little of Aunt Shiphra, who usually sent Mara to fetch water. Whenever I saw my cousin we would always ask if the other had heard news, but there was none. The boys had simply disappeared.

Towards the end of my first month of marriage, Shoshanna was preparing to tell our neighbour, Ide, about my pregnancy – thus informing the entire village – when I started to bleed. Shoshanna called for Auntie Shiphra, who boiled me a special tea and said that I must rest, but still the bleeding continued and then the cramps started. They got worse during the night, and finally I stumbled out, moaning and clutching my belly, to the unclean place. I squatted over the hole, feeling an urgency to pass water, but the trickle had the metallic smell of blood. Then there was a sudden gush and I felt something tearing away from inside me. I cried in pain, clutching my belly. Then a further gush and something slipped and snagged and tore out of me, making a dull splash as it fell into the pit below. I knew that I had lost my baby.

I stayed squatted, weeping, until Shoshanna came to find me. She lifted up a lamp and saw the blood spattered around the hole in the ground. Gently, she helped me up and helped me to the kitchen area where she warmed water and then washed me, wiping away the blood and other bits.

Ishmael was not so tender. "You tricked me into this marriage with a baby that isn't even there," he said as he stalked past at dawn to let the sheep out.

"Please, can I go and visit my sister for a few days?" I asked Shoshanna tearfully. I felt so desperately alone.

"Rivka has been doing your share of the housework for long enough," was her reply. The only place I could mourn for my baby was in the unclean place, where there were still brown stains around the hole where my blood had dried. Here I would weep silently, clutching the emptiness of my belly.

Any ongoing speculation over our speedy marriage soon died out when no announcement of a pregnancy was forthcoming. Although this improved our moral standing within the community, Ishmael seemed to feel that the loss of the baby was God's punishment upon us. He avoided me, and even after the bleeding had fully stopped and he could enter me again, he now approached it as a duty rather than something he took pleasure in.

Once, I stood at the compound door and watched him walk out with his flock. Imma was further down the street with her hand steadying the water jug on her shoulder and her back to us. I saw the way Ishmael looked at her, and knew that he had no desire to be my husband. Not long after that the beatings started.

There would always be a reason. Usually it was some slight I had given Rivka or Shoshanna, and the beatings were administered with their tacit approval. Only once, when Ishmael raised his hand to punch me in the face, did Shoshanna intervene. "No, not her face," she said, staring at her son. "What would people say?"

If I sobbed too loudly or wailed for my mother, as I did after the first time, Shoshanna would help me to my feet, or offer me a rag dipped in water, and say, "Really, Mariam, you must try harder not to provoke him," because the beatings were always my fault.

So, that's why it's so important that I don't lose this baby now. I can't afford to lose two. I'm squatting in the vegetable patch, weeding, when I feel a wave of cramps wash over me. I try to still my breathing and calm the fear roiling inside. I breathe slowly and the cramps subside. I keep breathing deeply and steadily, not daring to change position even a bit. Finally, I think everything is alright and that the danger has passed, but then I feel a thick trickle down my inner thigh and I know it's blood.

"Please, no," I gasp, as I clamber to my feet, which is a mistake, because this just makes the bleeding worse. I stumble into the unclean place and squat over the hole just in time as, with a strangled cry, I unclench my muscles and everything spills out. I remain squatting there, weeping in pain, and also because my hope for someone who might love me and for the beatings to stop has just disappeared into that hole, leaving just the drip, drip of what's still left inside. Gradually I still my breathing, and then manage to haul myself upright. There is blood around the pit hole, and I force myself to fetch a bowl of water and wash it away.

Ishmael is out with the flock, and Rivka and Shoshanna have gone to celebrate with one of the girls on our street who is getting ready for her wedding. They locked the compound door before they left to make sure I wouldn't go wandering. Quickly, my thoughts move from the life of my baby to my own life and how I am to survive this. There is no time for mourning. I realize what I must do. I'm able to clean myself up and strap a cloth stuffed with rags between my legs as the bleeding still hasn't fully stopped. I shrug out of my tunic and change into a clean one, bundling the bloodstained one up and hiding it in the inner room. I'll have to wash it later at the brook.

By the time Shoshanna and Rivka return, I've hidden all traces of the incident, but I'm exhausted and am lying down.

"You call that weeding?" said Rivka, looking at the first row and a half, which was all I achieved.

"I'm sorry," I say. "I felt sick and I had to lie down."

"Is everything alright with the baby?" asks Shoshanna. I nod. "Here, we brought you some herb-filled pastries from the celebration," she adds.

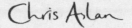

I thank her and nibble at them. I wonder how long I'll be able to keep up this lie before they realize the truth. I'm really not sure what to do, except that they mustn't find out, and that gives me a little time to come up with some kind of plan.

The next day I feel a little better and manage to add my tunic to the load of washing I take down to the brook. As I work the crusted stains out of the tunic, I imagine myself letting the baby go on the waters, being taken by God and the currents, and I try to sob as quietly as possible. I'm still bleeding a bit, but it grows less. My appetite returns and I'm feeling much better physically, but at the same time I'm paralysed with fear. What will Ishmael do when he finds out? Rivka is losing patience with me too and, although I'm still weak, I offer to resume my water-carrying duties. All it takes is one word from her and our secret is out and then who knows what will happen? That night, while Ishmael curls himself against me, all I can imagine is his hands around my throat, choking me, as he curses me for being unable to give him a child.

I wake up the next morning and all I can think about is this fear. I'm paralysed by it and can't think of any way out. I'm finding it harder to breathe and I even think about running away, but what would people say? I couldn't bring more shame on my sister.

Over breakfast, my distracted thoughts are interrupted by pounding on the compound door. I go to answer it, adjusting my headscarf, as Young Shimon bursts through.

"Quick," he says to Ishmael. "Halfai needs you. You're to be one of the witnesses to the confession."

Without further explanation, Shimon dashes out and Ishmael looks at us, shrugs, and then follows him.

"Mariam, isn't it time you went to fetch water?" says Shoshanna, and I know she wants me to find out more. "In fact, I've been meaning to get the strap on these sandals fixed," she adds. "I'll come with you."

I'll be surprised if Tauma the cobbler has set up his stall so early. The village square is still largely shadowed, the sun yet to crest the olive hills to the east, but as it turns out, there are more people about than usual at this time of day. We spot several elders hurrying purposefully towards the prayer house, and at the well there doesn't seem to be much drawing of water.

"Shoshanna, have you heard?" asks a plump woman with wide eyes, eager to share the story with a newcomer. Shoshanna shakes her head and the woman continues. "You know Hillel, the date merchant who lives on the street that leads to the brook? Well, he's been up north selling dates and olives and sent word that he'd return next week. Well, it turns out he was able to get home sooner and decided to travel through the night to surprise his wife first thing in the morning. And a surprise is what everyone gets!"

"That slut Rohel had taken another man to bed!" interrupts a forceful older lady, ignoring the plump woman's annoyance. "The adulterer managed to escape – naked as the day he was born, by all accounts – and now she won't say who he was. Hillel was in such a rage. He dragged her before Halfai and now they're questioning her."

I realize whose daughter they're talking about and feel the blood drain from my face. "Here," I say to Shoshanna, and thrust the empty water jug into her hands. "I have to go."

I've never been to her house but I know roughly where it is. When I get to her street I'm directed by the sounds of wailing. The compound door is open and I pause for a moment but then just walk in, uninvited.

Elisheba rocks backwards and forwards, held by the same women I joked and laughed with up at the sheep spring. "Please God," she cries. "What have I done to deserve this?"

"I just heard," I say, and the women look up and shift a little so that I can join them. "I'm so sorry." What other words are there?

Elisheba rages one moment, saying things like, "I'd kill her myself, that dog, that whore! How could she disgrace us like this?" and then she's filled with love and hurt, and sobs, "My poor baby, what have you done? What will they do to you?"

"Where is her other daughter?" I whisper to one of the neighbour ladies.

"Sholum is staying with Elisheba's cousin – the one with the sandal stall. We took Rohel's daughter there, too. They're taking it in turns to ride around the compound on the camel. Best that they know as little as possible," she says.

My heart goes out to these little girls who will both be tainted by Rohel's decision.

Other women arrive. There are no men and I realize that Elisheba's father must have been called to the interrogation. I notice that I'm the youngest there, so I boil water and pick some sprigs of mint and chamomile from Elisheba's herb garden to make tea.

Shoshanna and the plump gossip eventually turn up and they, too, start to weep as they see Elisheba's distress, forgetting the glee with which they had so recently digested the news. Shoshanna notices me, and looks puzzled, as if unsure whether to be angry with me or not for coming and helping. She shrugs and I'm guessing she's decided that I'm making her look good.

A self-important youth comes to the compound door and shouts, "They're coming out of the prayer house now. Halfai will announce the verdict in the square."

Of course he will. That man never misses the opportunity for a rapt audience. Elisheba struggles to her feet, the other women hauling her up, and they move as a mass towards the compound door. I decide to tidy up a little before joining them, and help myself to some of the leftover tea and some flatbread and curds. They seem to have forgotten that Halfai always likes to preach a sermon before releasing the news that people really want to hear.

Sure enough, by the time I've made my way to the square, it's packed with people and Halfai is ranting. They've placed some large planks across the well and Halfai is standing on them, turning the well into an impressive platform. I can't help hoping the planks break.

"Remember Nadab and Abihu: holy men who burnt incense incorrectly. What happened? The Lord's fire blazed over them and consumed them. This is how the Lord deals with the sons of Aaron. How much more does his rage blaze now?"

There are shouts of encouragement that come from one quarter of the crowd in particular. I stand on tiptoe and see that it is Hillel, surrounded by his friends. He has ash on his head and his robe is torn. I stop listening and crane my head to see Rohel. I've spoken with her sometimes at the well, but she's older than me and we were never friends. I can't see her anywhere, but I can hear Elisheba moaning and weeping, even though her back's to me. Young Shimon and Ishmael stand on either side of Halfai; his henchmen. The elders are all stood around the platform.

Significantly, there is no man bound. This must mean that Rohel still hasn't given the name of the man she was with. Or youth? It could be anybody. I wonder for a moment if Ishmael left my side during the night and slipped out unnoticed. It really wouldn't surprise me.

There is a commotion and Rohel is dragged out of the prayer house. Her face is bruised and there is a cut on her forehead. I don't know if that was Hillel's doing or part of the interrogation. Elisheba shrieks and surges forward, hands gripping her and holding her back on all sides. Women around her wail and men around Hillel shout, "Whore!"

Rohel keeps her eyes on the ground as she is pushed and shoved forward. A space opens up for her in front of the platform, elders beating the crowd back. She stands there until one of the elders kicks the back of her legs and then she falls into a kneeling position.

"This is your last chance to rid this village of corruption," says Halfai. "Redeem yourself now, before the village you've disgraced."

Rohel keeps her head bowed and is silent.

"Will you say nothing?" Halfai demands, and for a crowd we're pretty silent, everyone wanting to hear. The silence hangs in the air for a few moments, and then Halfai announces, "Take her outside the village," and the crowd erupts into shouts, cheers, and wailing.

Halfai is helped down from the platform by Young Shimon and they are all buoyed along as the whole village surges down the street which leads to the brook. As we pass it, youths and young men stop to collect stones, testing their heft and weight and discussing amongst themselves whether a smooth, heavy stone with more chance of accuracy is better than a jagged one which would inflict more damage. I see Ishmael and Shimon pause to join them.

We pass the date palms where I used to meet my father and move into the wilderness, until Halfai tells the crowd to stop. We are now just outside the official village border. Even though there has never been a stoning in our village during my lifetime, people seem to know instinctively what to do. The women gather around Elisheba, wailing. The men form a rough semi-circle around Rohel. There is some position-changing, with those skilled with a sling, such as Ishmael, given prime spots. Some of the younger boys are pushing and laughing, but all are silenced as Halfai raises a hand. He prays that this cleansing of an evil stain will purify our village. Standing beside Rohel, he looks almost fatherly.

When he has finished, Elisheba cries out in the silence, "Rohel, my darling girl. Don't look at them; just look at me." She manages to smile through her tears. "I'm here, my child. Just look at me."

Rohel's face crumples as she looks to her mother, and she begins to weep. Halfai walks backwards with his hand still raised. Hillel is pushed to the front of the crowd and given what is considered a good stone for throwing, and placed nearest his disgraced wife. An older, tear-stained man – Rohel's father – is also pushed forward and handed a stone, which he drops, falling to his knees.

"That's it; keep looking at me," says Elisheba to her daughter. She has been allowed to move to the front of the women. Halfai looks at the men and then lowers his hand as if to start a race, and the rocks fly. I see Ishmael judge the weight of his rock – a jagged one – take aim and throw it hard and straight. He smiles slightly as it hits the target and again the fear blooms in my stomach of what he could do to me; what those strong, sure hands could do. I keep my eyes on my husband. I don't want to watch Rohel die, but I can't help but hear it.

Her last cry is cut short, as if she's winded. Some of the rocks clatter against the rocky ground, missing their mark. Others make a deep thump as they connect with the softer parts of her body, or a crack where they hit her skull. I hear her stumble and fall to the ground. I turn to look as Elisheba shrieks and is held back by the women around her. For a moment I can't see anything because I am blinded by tears. I blink them away and see Halfai bending over Rohel, holding her wrist, checking for a pulse. "No," he says. "She is still alive. Aim for the head."

The men collect their stones, some wiping blood off them, or even splinters of bone. They gather closer this time, lifting the rocks above their heads. At Halfai's command, the rocks rain down. There is a moment of silence where even Elisheba is quiet. Halfai disappears from my view and then I hear him announce, "It is done."

With a groan, Elisheba rushes forward, flinging men out of her way, and collapses over her daughter, cradling her in her arms, and then beating her own breast and face, and throwing handfuls of dust over her head. Elisheba's husband stumbles forward, too, but faints before he gets to the body. At first the young men mill aimlessly, unsure what to do now that the killing is done. Then someone suggests a swim to clean off the blood, and that's where they head.

"But where can we bury her?" I hear a man asking Halfai anxiously, as Halfai strides back towards the village.

"Anywhere outside the village and outside the village tombs," says Halfai.

"I'm just glad her brother never lived to see her disgrace," I hear Ishmael saying to Shimon as they walk past me.

"I think your stone might have been the killer shot," Shimon replies. "You've always been on target."

Ishmael claps him on the shoulder, leaving a bloody handprint. "Oh, sorry," he says, and they laugh.

What kind of son would Ishmael have given me? I'm suddenly relieved that my womb is empty. For a moment, disgust overcomes my fear of him. I don't know how I can go back to his home tonight. I'm not sure it's even possible. I look for Marta but can't see her. Then I spot her and some of the women from our street gathered under one of the date palms in prayer. They're praying for Elisheba and for her family. I wait until they are finished, wondering why they pray to the God who apparently commanded this stoning in the first place.

Marta sees me and we embrace tearfully, holding each other for a long time. Everyone is feeling quite emotional right now. It feels so good to be held by another, not because they want something from me but just because they love me. "Marta, I'm going to come by tonight," I say. I'm on the verge of making a decision that I haven't consciously acknowledged.

Marta beams. "Shoshanna gave you permission?"

"It will probably be after sundown," I say, avoiding her question. First there's something I must do. I turn back to the village and make it to Elisheba's house before her husband is carried back by the men from their street. As I had suspected, sounds of indignant braying come from within their stable. I find a donkey inside and feed him a few handfuls of parched grain, and empty some more into a cloth bag which I add to his saddlebags along with a water-skin half filled with what's left in the water jar. I pause and drink the last of the cold tea before I go. When it was still warm, Rohel was still alive.

By the time I've returned to the stoning spot, the only people left are four of Elisheba's closest neighbours and relatives. Elisheba has curled herself around Rohel's body and croons gently to her, stroking her blood-matted hair.

The neighbours look up, questioningly. "Isn't that Elisheba's donkey?" one of them says.

I nod, pulling out another handful of grain to feed it. "They won't let her be buried with our dead, but I remember my father once told me about the place where lepers are buried. We can be there and back before sundown."

"Buried with lepers?" the neighbour spits in disdain.

I shrug and don't take offence. It slowly dawns on the women that there really aren't any other options if we want to avoid an unmarked grave by a roadside. "Wait for us," say two of the women, who hurry back to the village and return a little while later with a linen shroud and a collection of bulging cloth pouches.

"Come." They gently lift Elisheba. "We must honour her with a decent burial."

One of the women covers Rohel's face with a headscarf; I help another woman with Rohel's legs while others lift the arms. The body is cooling but still pliable.

"I've never been there, but Father used to come from over there." I point towards a low outcrop of rocks. I'm given the donkey's tether, and lead the group while others support Elisheba, who finds walking a struggle. We get to the outcrop and there's a path we discover there, which we follow.

By noon we see our first leper. She looks startled and a little wary of us. "You must have lost your way," she says. "This is leper territory."

We ask for directions and eventually we find the caves where the lepers are buried. There are no family caves, like in our village. The leper has walked with us, always staying well in front, and leads us to a cave that has not been used for some time, where there'll be less risk to us of contagion.

I stay with the donkey, the leper and the corpse while the other women enter the cave and lay down salt and the shroud. Then we

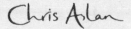

carry Rohel in. I'm thirsty – I'm sure we all are in this heat – but all the water in the water-skin is used to wash the corpse. I go back outside for this; I've seen enough bruised flesh of my own.

I find a spot of shade beside one of the larger rocks and crouch in it, the leper having wandered off after I'd given her a few carrots I found in the saddlebags. My head begins to pound because I need water, but I take a strange pleasure in the pain, seeing it as part of my service and solidarity to Elisheba. It suddenly occurs to me that this is probably the furthest I've ever been from our village.

I must have dozed because I wake with a start as the women emerge from the cave. The shade has grown as the sun descends, and we help Elisheba onto the donkey. The saddlebags are stained with dried blood but we are all beyond caring, and trudge wearily back to the village. The sun has almost set by the time we draw near, and the whole village shimmers in a mirage of heat from the wilderness beneath our feet. I try to steer us at an angle so that we'll hit the main road. It's not the quickest way and one woman frowns until she realizes that I wish to bypass the stoning place.

"Your mother-in-law will be wondering where you are," says one of Elisheba's neighbours as we leave the main road and trudge into the village. "You've been a great blessing to her. She'll remember this," she adds, and I realize I'm being dismissed.

I pause for a moment, torn between the well and the brook. First I choose the well, asking one of the younger girls to pour water for me, and splashing it into my hands and then gulping it down, greedily. One of the women from our street gives me a look that says, "Does your mother-in-law know you're wandering around outside without a water jug?" I ignore it, and head back to the brook, finding the women's bathing spot behind the reeds empty. I strip off and sink into the water, washing my hair even though I have no soap.

The air is still warm when I emerge, and I shake out the dust in my tunic before putting it on. I feel strangely calm and at peace. I still haven't formally acknowledged my decision to myself.

Back at my childhood home, I don't knock on the compound door, but take a running jump at the apricot branch and haul myself over.

"Miri, you gave me a fright," says Marta as I land in our compound garden. "Here, the yogurt and mint is ready and there's lentil stew in the pot. You can help me with the flatbreads."

We work together in a companionable silence that I have missed so much it almost makes me cry. When the flatbreads are steaming, we sit down to eat. Marta is so good at giving me space to speak when I'm ready. I see that she's tidied up the compound for my arrival and even washed her hair.

"I have news," I say, after wolfing down the meal.

"I know," Marta beams. "I saw Shoshanna this morning and she told me that you're with child." She squeezes my hand. "I'm so glad things seem to be improving."

I shake my head. "I lost it," I say quietly. "I just keep losing them."

I don't have time to say anything more, because Marta clutches me in a fierce embrace. I feel myself slacken as I lean into my older sister and realize just how wrung out I feel. We sit huddled together for a while before Marta studies me, reading my face, and brushes a strand of my hair away. "How did Ishmael take it?" she asks.

"I was terrified of telling him," I explain. "He started beating me after I lost the last one."

"That dog!" says Marta, looking murderous. "Miri, why didn't you say something? I'll tell Shoshanna that if this happens again I will go directly to Halfai, and this is no idle threat."

"No," I say gently, trying to soothe her. "There's no need."

Marta looks as if she wants to protest, but one of the things I've always loved about my sister is the way she can hold her tongue. She waits and I explain.

"Every day I knew I was with child, I was so worried I'd lose

Chris Aslan

it. My whole body was clenched, and even at night I worried that if I relaxed, the baby might somehow come out." I pause, trying to find the right words. "I lost it anyway, but I'm still clenched. I think I've felt clenched ever since he raped me. I'm constantly terrified that Rivka will say something or that Ishmael will find an excuse to beat me. I don't think I can live like this any more. Marta, I'm not going back there. Ever."

Marta is stunned and I give her a moment to digest this news.

"But Miri, what will people say?" she asks. "Think of the gossip and the shame on our household. Let me speak to Shoshanna."

"No," I say, more loudly than I meant. "You don't know how alone I've felt. I won't go back. Please, Marta, if you love me…" I falter and begin to weep.

"Oh Miri," says Marta, taking me in her arms. "This will always be your home, too. I have also felt so alone."

I can't speak. We both just cry, clutching each other tightly, and remain that way for quite a while.

Chapter Eight

"Tell her to come out here and speak to my face," Ishmael snarls outside our compound door.

"Please, Ishmael, her decision has been made. I'll ask my aunt to speak to your mother tomorrow," Marta calls back.

"She's not leaving; she carries my child." He has an edge to his voice and I wonder if he'll try climbing over the wall.

"No, she doesn't, Ishmael. She lost it."

We hear him swearing and then he kicks the door hard.

"I never pleased you," I call out softly, not wanting to antagonize him further. "Now you can have Imma."

He swears at me. "You'll pay for this," he adds, and we hear him leave.

Marta gives me a look.

"I know," I say. "It's going to be a challenge."

"This is just the start. You might be shunned by the whole village."

Marta lets out a long breath and then looks up at the night sky. "Come on," she says.

It's a warm evening and we drag a seating mat up the ladder to the flat roof and lie on our backs watching the stars.

"You know you're never going to get back any of your dowry," she says after a while.

"Well, they actually paid for most of it. Anyway, I still have this." I wince as I remove the gold ring in my nose – the symbol of a married woman. "I'll sell it tomorrow. I won't be needing it any more." I stretch back and look at the stars, and for a moment I feel queasy and upside down, as if I'll fall upwards and into the never-ending basin above me. "And they can keep their 'new' tunics," I say, and sense Marta smiling in the dark. "This has been such a costly mistake," I sigh. "And I know it's cost you, too."

"Shh," says Marta.

"If I'd known El would just abandon you like that – "

"Shh," she says again. I'm quiet and we watch the stars. Every now and then one of them falls in a glittering trail.

"You know, this morning it would never have occurred to me to leave him. It was when I saw him with the stone in his hand and the way he looked at Rohel. That was when, in my heart, I knew what to do. I couldn't stay and let him hurt me again."

We're silent for a while.

"Marta, I can't help thinking about the other man, whoever he was. Right now he's eating his supper or he's talking to his wife or to his mother. They're probably discussing the stoning. Tomorrow he'll wake up with the rest of his life ahead of him."

"Who are you talking about?"

"Whoever was in Rohel's bed this morning. She didn't name him. He probably made sure he was in the front row of the stone-throwers to avoid suspicion. Now he's having his supper and Rohel's body lies in a lepers' grave."

"It's terrible, but she knew the law as well as we do," Marta says gently.

"Yes, but the law is meant for justice. How was this justice?"

Marta says nothing. After a while I say, "Marta, when I saw Elisheba today, it reminded me of how we were when Father was

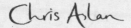

driven out. She was so – so broken." I turn to Marta in the dark. "Could you pray for Elisheba?"

"Of course," she says softly, and we sit up and raise our hands. "But you know her better. Why don't you pray?"

"No," I say. I don't try to explain, but I don't think I'll be praying again.

The next day I lift my mother's water jug onto my shoulder, enjoying its familiar heft. I hadn't realized I missed it. At the well the stoning is still the main topic of gossip, but Shoshanna has already begun her work. Several ladies spot me and then ostentatiously turn their backs. I've experienced plenty of pity before, but this disdain is new. Part of me wants to tell them what really happened, but I know they won't listen. I fill my jar, ignoring their whispers. I avoid eye contact, but I won't bow my head or scurry away.

At home, Aunt Shiphra and Heras, Halfai's wife, sit uncomfortably together while Marta busies herself preparing mint tea and doing anything else that will keep her from having to sit down with them.

"We've been waiting for you," Heras states the obvious. I greet them, put the jar in its place, and come and join them on the mats.

"I see you've removed your nose-ring." Heras sniffs with disapproval.

"I plan to sell it," I say, holding her gaze.

"Sell it?" Aunt Shiphra interrupts. "What do girls know of gold? You'll do no such thing. Here, give it to me. I'll make sure you get a good price for it." I shoot her a grateful look as Heras purses her lips.

"I don't want my dowry back," I say. "They can keep the sheep. I just want to be left alone."

"'Alone' is the correct word. No honest man will ever take a used woman like you as his wife. What possible future could you have without Ishmael? He's a good man. I've spoken to

Alabaster

Shoshanna. Of course everyone is shaken up after yesterday, but if she sees you're fully repentant – "

"Auntie," I interrupt, "I'm not. He beat me. Look for yourself." I make to remove my tunic. "Some of the bruises still haven't faded."

Heras shakes her head in impatience. "Yes, yes. Shoshanna mentioned Ishmael occasionally losing his temper, but you must serve him well and not antagonize him."

"I won't go back."

"You must. It's your duty."

"I won't."

"No wonder he beats you," she mutters. "How do you propose to live? I can tell you now that if there's any whoring in this village – well, you saw what happened yesterday."

"It's not your concern. I'll live here with my sister. Is there a law against that?"

"Arrangements like this lead our men astray. Why can't you see sense and return to your husband? It's where you belong."

"Was there anything else?" I ask, and refuse to lower my gaze.

"Pah!" says Heras, and clambers to her feet. "I'm glad your father never lived to see you bring such disgrace to this household." She turns before walking out. "You will be shunned."

And that is what happens. Now everyone treats me like Imma does. They stare through me as if I'm an apparition, the stallholders refuse to serve me, and I must depend on market day and traders from outside the village in order to make my purchases. Marta is still reluctant to leave the compound, so I learn to plan better, buying all we need on market day, or giving coins to Cousin Mara to make purchases for me.

This shunning should bother me, but I prefer it to the constant fear I lived under with Ishmael. It was like holding my breath all the time and now I've let it out and can take fresh air into my lungs. I get lewd calls from some of the young men, but ignore them.

However, there is still the question of how we are to survive. Aunt Shiphra sits me and Marta down, wanting to know how we intend to keep a roof over our heads. Usually we'd have brined olives in storage to sell over the course of the year, but I brined none before my hasty marriage, and the fresh olives Marta was forced to sell at harvest-time, during the glut, didn't leave her with much. Our situation really isn't good.

"I'm helping Marta with the carpet business," I say.

"That's a grand term for one loom. Marta was barely able to feed herself when she was alone. What will you do with two mouths to feed?"

Marta glances at me and I know she's wondering if we should mention the jar. I give an almost imperceptible shake of my head. "We still have the olive groves," I say.

"Oh, so you plan to go up there and get raped again?" Shiphra snorts. She has a point. So far I've experienced only lecherous comments from men of the village. Who knows what might happen up in the groves?

"There's no man in the household to speak for you," Aunt Shiphra continues. "Halfai is furious. Marta, who'll buy your carpets now that Mariam's shunned? Yoezer won't risk upsetting Halfai, even if he is your relative."

"God will provide," I say, hoping this pious answer will silence her, but wondering the same thing myself.

"Just like he miraculously cured my brother?" Shiphra arches her eyebrows. "You need to do better than that."

"You're right," I say. "We do."

I start by forcing myself to sit at the loom, trying not to be dreadful. Balls of spun yarn hang from branches of the tree above us. The apricots are almost ripe. I look forward to harvesting them because it will be time well spent that doesn't involve weaving, and at least that's one thing we can eat. Marta can picture the carpet design in her head, but I can't, and she still has to remove one or two knots where I've used the wrong colour in the wrong place. I manage without too many mistakes for an hour or two, and then I straighten my neck and click my back, which are both sore from crouching over the loom.

"You're losing your concentration," she says, and we stop.

"Marta, we both know I'm a hopeless weaver, but I still think I can help."

Marta cocks her head but I won't say more. Instead we make herb-filled pastries and I take a plateful to Elisheba's. I've waited a little while, expecting that neighbours and relatives will have fussed over her during this first week of bereavement. She is subdued but grateful for a visit. Apparently I'm the only one who isn't a relative or neighbour who's come by, and she suspects that she, too, is being shunned. She hasn't left her compound since Rohel was stoned. Nor has her daughter, Sholum, or Rohel's daughter, Marta.

"Hillel threw her out," Elisheba whispers to me loudly, pointing at the girl. "He said, 'How do I even know she's mine?' So now I have both of them refusing to leave the compound and getting under my feet."

"At least they have each other," I say. They seem around the same age; they must be nine or ten years old.

"Better shunned than stoned," Elisheba tells me, after she's heard my news. "Rohel was not happy with Hillel. I told her that happiness in marriage isn't important. He put a roof over her head and gave her a daughter. She ran home once, wanting to leave him, but I made her go back." She sighs and wipes tears from her eyes. The two girls watch us solemnly.

I have an idea.

The next day I go down to the well with my jar. As usual, women turn their backs on me. Most of them take real delight in the shunning. I think it makes them feel better about themselves. Once my jar is filled, I head to the leatherwork stall, where saddles are stacked and sandals are piled into different sizes.

"Good morning, Uncle Tauma," I say.

He looks around quickly to see who's watching, but then returns my greeting. As I'd hoped, he's chosen not to shun me.

"I heard what you did for my cousin," he says, referring to Elisheba. "Thank you for helping her in her time of need."

"I hear that she's shunned, too."

"Only by those who know no better," he says, and I smile.

"I've come to you for help." He raises an eyebrow. "How often do you go to the capital?"

"Once or twice a month. I'm heading there tomorrow," he says. "Why?"

"How heavily laden is your camel?" I ask.

"Sometimes I take olives to press for oil, but usually it's only on the way back that I load her down."

"My sister weaves carpets," I explain. "They're good quality and knotted, not just flat-weave. Could I give you one to try to sell in the capital? Marta has several. They're not very heavy. We really need your help."

I see him weighing up the risks of helping a shunned woman. "Bring one to me," he says, turning away as if the conversation is finished. "I'll see what I can do. Bring it to my home and leave it with my wife."

I understand. He doesn't need trouble from Halfai, and already one or two people have begun to stare. I hurry home with my jar.

Two days later I visit his stall again in the heat of the afternoon when few customers are around. Good news: he sold the carpet and got a price higher than our relative Yoezer usually pays Marta for the larger sizes. "People in the capital have money," says Tauma, clinking coins into my hand. "And that Yoezer has been robbing you with the price he paid your sister."

I thank him and hand one of the silver coins back.

"It's too much," he says.

"I hope we can do business again. Can I drop off the other completed rugs at your compound this evening?"

When I get home and tell Marta the news, she can't believe the price we got. "Like I said, I know I can't weave, but I can sell. Let me be responsible for that side of things. Also, I have another plan."

"A plan?"

"I think it's time that Master Marta started training some apprentices."

Marta isn't keen but then I tell her about the two little girls at Elisheba's, tainted by Rohel's sin and never likely to shake the stigma. "How will they ever find husbands, and what will they live on if they don't?"

Reluctantly, Marta agrees to a trial period of one carpet. I hug her and then head to Elisheba's. Now I just have to convince Elisheba and the girls.

I suggest the idea, and then Elisheba gives me a bone-crushing hug and begins to weep. Neither of the girls wants to leave the compound, though.

"What's this?" Elisheba thunders, clipping them both on the backs of their heads. "Our guest offers you the opportunity to learn a skill – to be able to walk around our village with your heads held high and to afford nice clothes – and you do this?" She mimics them both before giving them a withering look. Then she turns to me. "We will come just after sunrise. It's time for all of us to leave this compound."

The next day, true to her word, Elisheba and the girls arrive just as we're finishing breakfast. Elisheba looks determined, but also a little shaken. "Whenever someone wanted to speak to me, I just kept walking, telling them that my daughters are learning to be weavers and that we mustn't keep their master waiting."

"Then let me introduce you to your master, Marta," I say, as the girls look up solemnly.

Marta gets up and then crouches in front of the two girls. "Mmm," she says, feeling one of Sholum's spindly forearms. "Not much meat there. And you —" she gives the other girl a hard stare – "are going to be a problem. How can we have two Martas here? Eh? Mariam will call for Marta to come for midday meal and up you'll run and all my food will be gobbled up by the time she realizes it was you." The little girl smiles shyly but says nothing. "There's only one thing for it. From now on, you will be called Little Marta." Little Marta nods. "Now, let's begin."

Marta leads them over to the loom and sits them down on a mat, one on either side of her, while Elisheba and I watch. "You see these warp threads? They're all boring and brown, just like dirt. We have to make a garden grow amongst them. Look at all the colours we have up here to make flowers grow." She points at the coloured yarn hanging down from the branches, adjusting them to make sure that the girls can reach. "Just like a flower garden, our carpet will grow slowly," she says, and already the girls have forgotten us. "But not too slow," she adds with mock ferocity, rapping Sholum gently on the knuckles and causing a giggle.

I grab the water jug and walk with Elisheba down to the well. People stare at us – two disgraced women happily in conversation together; by unspoken agreement, we try extra hard to smile in the face of disapproval. "I will be back for the girls at sundown," she says as we part, and gives my hand a squeeze.

Sholum's dextrous little fingers are perfect for knotting, and she learns fast. Little Marta is slower but Marta is happy with her progress. Big Marta is such a good teacher that I even feel a twinge of jealousy. She's strict with the girls but also remarkably patient, coaxing excellence from them. She tells them stories about the origins of the design they're working on, and lets them watch her weave at her normal speed, so they know what to aim for.

The girls respond to her with a quiet obedience that soon solidifies into devotion. They call her "master" just like the boys on their street refer to their own teachers of carpentry or leatherwork.

"Yesterday was so boring," the apprentices tell Marta on the first day of the week. "We had to stay at home, and we missed you so much. We didn't want to rest. We just want to work on the carpet."

After the first few days, the girls start to arrive and leave without Elisheba. Often she sends them with a plate of food enough for all four of us. We try to make sure that the bowl never returns empty, and Marta also gives the girls a few cooking lessons.

I ask Aunt Shiphra to speak with one of the saddle-makers and a woman who weaves coloured linen to find out how much they pay their apprentices. Then I negotiate with Marta and we agree that the girls will work for free on the first three carpets, but that after that, if the quality of their work is good, they will receive a portion of every sale. Marta no longer talks about a trial period.

Marta has just one drop spindle and usually spends most of winter spinning wool for the summer weaving. Now, with the extra hands, she's worried we'll run out of wool. I speak to Tauma and on market day he introduces me to one of the traders. He agrees to bring spun and dyed wool next week for a good price. Tauma also knows the other camel owners in neighbouring villages, and I'm able to put in an order for soft camel down so we can weave some luxury carpets as well.

Marta starts the girls on a small carpet, knowing that at first they'll weave slowly. When it's cut from the loom, I feel extravagant and go down to the bird-seller in the market and return with two plump pigeons. We celebrate with meat. "Here, take this to your mother," Marta says, rolling up the carpet and handing it to her apprentices. "She should enjoy the first fruits of your labours."

"I thought I was in charge of business," I say, after the girls have left.

"You couldn't have sold that," says Marta, aghast. "It was full of mistakes. I wouldn't put my name to such a carpet, but Elisheba will love it."

Chris Aslan

Although Marta is busier than ever, now she takes more care over her appearance. Her hair has regained its sheen and the dark hollows under her eyes have disappeared.

"I'm thinking about expansion," I say that evening, as we boil up the pigeon bones to make broth. "Look at the difference we're making in the lives of these girls. There are so few opportunities for girls to learn a trade. I've been thinking about the upper room. We could finish it properly and then set up a couple of looms inside. That way you could weave in winter and spring as well."

Marta smiles. "You're good at weaving words," she says. "Certainly better than weaving anything else."

I pinch her, grinning. "Maybe it's time for us to finally put the jar to good use."

"No," she says. "Father gave it to us for our dowries, Miri. We can't just go and spend it on some fantasy."

"Look around you, Marta. Where are these husbands we're to marry? Why do we save for a future that will never happen? At least think about it and we can talk more in a few days."

The next day at the well, one of the women who are supposed to be shunning me informs me that Imma and Ishmael are betrothed. Of course, it comes as no surprise, but I still find it hard to mask my emotions. I try to work out why I feel so sad. Is it because I worry for Imma that Ishmael will beat her, or because I'm worried that he won't? In which case, what does that say about me?

The following morning at the well, there is a flurry of discussion. "Mariam, have you heard?" says another of the women who would usually shun me. "The occupiers have caught one of the militant leaders along with most of his army."

It seems that the rules of shunning don't apply when there's the possibility of giving me bad news.

"Yokkan and Eleazar might be amongst them," she continues, looking disappointed at my stony-faced response. "They might be nailed along with their leader."

"Whatever God wills," I say, heaving up the bucket.

123

Alabaster

"Did you hear that?" the woman says to another of the gossips. "She has no heart, that girl."

At home, I ask Marta to leave the apprentices for a moment and I tell her the news, figuring that she'll hear it from Cousin Mara or Aunt Shiphra soon enough. Marta clings to me and begins to weep.

"Listen, we don't even know which group they joined," I say, trying to comfort her. "There are so many insurgent groups now."

"I pray for them every morning and every night," she sobs.

"That's all you can do," I whisper. After the way Eleazar abandoned her, I really don't care if he's alive or not.

The rest of the day is subdued. I spend it turning the drying apricots on our roof for the last time, and then at sunset inspect each one for worms before tying them up in a sack. After the apprentices have left, Marta busies herself cooking and shoos me away when I try to help. Instead, I climb the ladder to the upper room with the sack of dried apricots. We use the upper room mainly for storage. I stop and survey the mud-brick walls, unfinished beams and the uneven and unplaned floorboards, trying to guess what it might cost to renovate. I'm still lost in thought when there is a knock at the compound door. I hear Marta answer it and I assume it must be Shiphra or Mara, come to discuss the news of the captured militia leader.

Instead, there's a shriek and then Marta is weeping. It must be news about Yokkan and Eleazar. I swallow, giving myself a moment to prepare for the news, but then, as I climb down the ladder, Marta is laughing. "Miri! Come quick!"

It's dusk and the visitor below is in shadow. I clatter down the remaining rungs and almost collide with the young man below, falling into his arms. It's not Eleazar. I know him, but I can't think where from.

"It's me, Mariam," he says, grinning. Why can I not place him? Then I gasp with recognition and stumble back, trying to put distance between us.

124

"It's alright," says Malchus. "Look." He pulls back his robe where the leprous lesion once worked along his chin and jaw, creeping down to his shoulder blade. Now, the lesion is totally gone. His skin is smooth and healthy. "See? You don't need to be afraid or keep your distance," he says.

"How can this be?" I stammer, as Marta laughs and cries at the same time.

"He cured me!" Malchus says again. "I found the doctor and he cured me."

"But that's impossible! I don't understand."

"I know," he laughs. "But here I am."

"And Father?"

He shakes his head. "He got weaker each day until I had to carry him. By then I was weak, too, and could barely walk myself."

"Why wouldn't he take the stupid donkey?" I cry. Marta sits Malchus down and offers him a bowl of broth.

"Your father kept urging me to leave him behind, but how could I? He was like a father to me. We slept in a disused grave cave in some foothills. The next morning I woke and he was gone. I kept looking for him, but he'd hidden himself in one of the caves. I couldn't find him. I don't know what else I could have done."

"Was there a leper colony nearby?" Marta asks, clinging on to a last shred of hope. "A place where he could recover?"

Malchus shakes his head. "He didn't want me to find him. He knew that we would never make it to the doctor together." Malchus is whispering now, his voice heavy with emotion. "He died so I would have a chance to live."

"Oh, Father," I cry, and cling to Marta. We both weep and then so does Malchus. I don't want to believe this news, and part of me wishes Malchus had never returned so we could be left with a glimmer of hope.

"I was so sure he was still alive," Marta sobs eventually. "Every day I pray for Father and for the boys."

Malchus looks up, wiping his eyes.

"You mean Eleazar and Yokkan?" he says. We just stare at him stupidly. "Of course they're alive. That's what I've come to tell you."

Chapter Nine

This is too much for Marta, who continues to sob; joy and sorrow blended. I just feel weary. "Tell us about them," I say to Malchus.

"Well, after I was cured, I went home. First I saw the holy man and he inspected me and pronounced me clean. He conducted the cleansing rituals and then I returned to my father's house. At first they wouldn't let me in and thought I was a ghost, but then the whole street came out to see me and celebrate. They killed a sheep in my name and we all feasted. I was being given a second chance at life, but I couldn't live my old life again. How could I stay in the same town as my wife, who was now a mother to another man's children? Wherever I went, people wanted to touch me and poke me and show me to their friends. I just wanted to be normal. There were also debts I had to repay to your father. I knew I had to come back here and tell you about him. And I wanted to find the doctor. I knew I could never repay him, but I wanted to thank him properly for what he did.

"Wherever I went, he had been there just a day or so before. I kept missing him. By the time I caught up with him, a group of militants from the hills had come down to listen to him speak. When you hear him, you'll understand. Yokkan and Eleazar were with them, but after listening to the doctor, they decided not to rejoin the militants but to follow the doctor; to sit at his feet and to go where he goes."

"So they're both alive and well? They've not been injured?" Marta asks.

"They're both fine," Malchus smiles. "It won't be easy for them to return, especially Eleazar. He still feels shame at his behaviour towards you."

"Return here?" says Marta.

"I didn't tell them who I was. I'd never seen Eleazar before, and Yokkan only once. When I asked Eleazar about his parents, he told me they were both dead. I asked him if he had any other family and he said that he didn't, because he'd run away and now they would never want to see him again."

Maybe my brother isn't so stupid after all, I think to myself.

"How do you thank a man who is dead? How do you repay him with your gratitude? I kept thinking about this, and then I heard that the teacher planned to come down to the capital. I thought that maybe I could arrange for him to come here, and then you would be reunited with Eleazar."

"Wait, I'm confused," I say. "The teacher is the doctor? They're the same person?"

Malchus nods. "When the teacher heard that Eleazar and Yokkan had run away, of course he insisted that we come and visit. He sent me ahead so that you could prepare. They come tomorrow evening. Also, I want to give you this." He rummages in the cloth sack he's been carrying, and pulls out a small bag of coins. "When I left home, my father and brother gave me this. It should cover the costs of the teacher's time here."

Everything is moving too fast. "So, you're asking us to host the teacher who will come here tomorrow with Eleazar and Yokkan?"

"And the teacher's friends." Malchus nods and passes the bag to me. It's heavy with coins.

"Malchus, how much is in here? We can afford to feed the teacher and Eleazar and Yokkan ourselves. Aunt Shiphra will definitely help."

Malchus chuckles. "How much have you heard about the teacher?"

I look blank. I don't think he realizes that I'm shunned and don't hear anything from anyone down at the well.

"He's all anyone talks about. Surely you've heard something?" says Malchus. "Wherever he goes, he's mobbed. I was only able to get close to him because I was a leper and people had to get out of my way. Every day, more and more people are following him. It won't just be a few friends."

"And he wants to come here, to our house?" says Marta. "Shouldn't he stay with Halfai, our village holy man?"

"He wants to stay here," says Malchus. "It is a very great honour."

"How many people will come? Give me a number," says Marta.

"I don't know," Malchus replies unhelpfully. "Can your aunt host the overflow?"

"The overflow?" Marta looks pale. "Surely he won't want to stay in a leper's home. We don't have much of a reputation in our village."

"He doesn't care about stuff like that," says Malchus. He looks up at the night sky where a half-moon is rising. "And now, I should be getting back to the capital to let them know it's arranged."

"Go? But you've just got here. It's late," I say.

"I'll be fine. I need to let the teacher know that everything is ready. God willing, tomorrow you'll see your brother and cousin again."

After he's gone we just sit there, stunned, trying to take it all in. I can't stop thinking about Father, and then I wonder what it will be like to see Eleazar tomorrow. If only it was Father who was returning.

Alabaster

"He didn't even tell us how the teacher – the doctor – cured him," I say.

Marta is still lost in thought. "Empty the pouch," she says after a while. "We need to know how much we have. There's no way we can get the upper room ready by tomorrow evening, but we can put carpets up on the roof and I can move the loom and see if the neighbours will lend us more seating mats for guests down here. We'll need to borrow lamps. Would Elisheba be willing to bake bread for us? We're going to need a lot of bread. And we'll need at least one sheep."

I'm dispatched to talk to Elisheba, even though it's far too late for a woman to be wandering around outside alone. I have barely explained to her what has happened when she dispatches her husband next door to fetch one of her neighbours. Soon her other neighbours come out to see what's going on. They're the only women who won't shun me. As we talk, it turns out that I really am one of the few people in the village who haven't heard tales of the doctor. No one can believe that he's actually coming to our village. I foolishly mention that Malchus has given me money that we are to use to host the doctor, and soon Elisheba is talking about the feast and appointing various neighbours as bakers.

"Come here before sunrise with a sack of flour, a pouch of yeast, some salt. If you can find date syrup or honey in the market, then bring as much as they have, and butter," she tells me.

I leave, breathless. I want to go somewhere quiet and remember my father, but things are just as bad at home. Aunt Shiphra, Mara, and Marta are making mental lists of all that needs to be done and who should do what.

"We can't buy sheep from Ishmael," says Shiphra, looking pointedly at me. "But I can send Mara to that other shepherd boy, the one with the squint. We don't want to be shamed without enough meat for all the guests. In fact, we'll probably need two sheep. What do you think, Marta?" She glances up at the tree

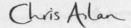

we're sitting under. "Such a shame the teacher didn't come a few weeks ago, during apricot season."

"We have a sack of dried ones," says Marta. "And isn't your neighbour's peach tree in fruit?"

"Good thinking," Aunt Shiphra beams.

They continue planning and I get drowsy, nodding off during a passionate exchange regarding pastries. When I wake up they're talking about Yokkan, who is now of marriageable age, wondering if he's changed. Marta reminisces about Eleazar, and I notice that all her stories are about before Father got sick. I get up quietly and go to the inner room. I lie down and think about Father. I imagine how it would have been if he'd come striding into our compound this evening, with no limp and no leprosy. I imagine him sweeping us up in his arms and me burying myself in his chest and beard, inhaling the smell of him. Then I cry myself to sleep.

It's still dark when Marta rouses me. Mara and Shiphra are already up. It seems they stayed the night. Marta starts rattling off a list of what I'm to do, but I stop her. "Let me start by drawing water, and then you can tell me what to do next," I say. We're clearly not bothering with breakfast today.

I'm still a little groggy as I stumble down to the well, hoping to savour a solitary moment before the business of today starts. There's a cluster of women already there, well before dawn, and they mob me.

"Is it true?" they clamour. "When is the doctor coming? Do you know how much he costs? Did he really cure your father's friend? Does he also cure women?"

I stammer, trying to answer their questions, although I feel I know less than anyone else about this man.

"It's such a great honour that he should come to our little village," says one of the elder wives, who until today was ostentatiously shunning me. "Shouldn't we lay down rush mats

131

and carpets around the prayer house and host him there? He won't want to visit a leper's house."

I shrug. "Apparently he's very keen to visit our house," I say, "but don't feel that *you* have to."

She splutters at my rudeness, but quite frankly, I prefer being shunned to being mobbed, and just want to be left alone. By the time I've filled my jar, more women have arrived, and I'm surrounded by a clamour of questions, few of which I know the answer to. I grab the jar, spilling it in my haste to get home.

"Mariam, wait." I feel a hand on my shoulder. It's Cyria, Crazy Mariam's mother, and she's weeping.

"Walk with me," I say gently, wanting to get away from the square. Once we're up the street we pause.

"Is it true?" she whispers.

"You mean about the doctor coming?" I say.

She nods.

"Yes, yes, it is."

"Do you think he would see my daughter? I know she's not good with crowds. Maybe I could tie her up. I promise we wouldn't take up much of his time." I can see the desperation in her eyes.

"Please, come tonight, Auntie; be our guest. You're always welcome in our house."

This just makes her weep more. "Thank you," she whispers, and bends down, and I'm aghast when I realize she means to kiss my feet.

"Stop!" I almost drop my jar as I reach down to help her back up. "What is this?" She's sobbing uncontrollably now, and I try to hold her and my water jar in an uncomfortable and wet embrace.

She wipes her nose on the hem of her tunic and sniffs. "You must think me a foolish old woman," she says, smiling.

"Of course not, Auntie Cyria. I think you're very brave and that Mariam is blessed to have such a loving mother."

She nods absently. "I must go now," she says. "I'll bring curds

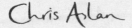

Chris Aslan

tonight, and I'll bring a jar of spiced olive oil. You'll need a lot of oil to anoint the guests, as well as for the lamps."

She's right, and I wonder if Marta has thought of this. I look down at the water jar and wonder how long it will last before I have to fetch more.

Sure enough, as soon as I arrive I'm called to pour water over cut vegetables and there's not much left to pour into our main storage jar. This time I'm sent with Mara, who also has a jar with her. We face the clamour of women and even men wanting to know what they can bring to the feast, brazenly inviting themselves. Mara almost falls on our way back, as we hurry away from the crowd.

The compound is just as bad. Aunt Shiphra has taken to guarding the compound door, as Marta looks too harried. Elisheba has sent the apprentices to help, along with some other girls from her street, and I notice that several of our neighbours who were supposed to be shunning us have turned up and now willingly take orders from Marta. Mingled with the sounds of sweeping, the clatter of pots, and the issuing of orders, I hear the indignant bleating of two rams, tied to the apricot tree and straining to reach Marta's herb patch.

"Miri!" I'm summoned, and Marta gives me a handful of coins and reels off a list of what I am to buy, in extravagant quantities. "You'd better take Mara with you in case they shun you," she says.

I'm grateful for the help, although I'm pretty sure that our shunning days are over. I'm proved right as we enter the first stall to buy honey, date syrup, pomegranate molasses, and flour. I've never purchased flour before – we mill our own grain – or such large quantities of these extravagant luxuries. Nor have I ever been treated so well. Mara and I struggle not to smile as old Daoud empties his stores for us, offering to deliver our purchases to the door, and using clean new sacking to wrap each bundle.

"I have some mountain honey which I keep at home," he says. "Much too precious to have here and only for the best, the very best. Of course, I would never dream of selling it, but I will bring it as a gift to the doctor this evening."

I thank him and wonder how we'll accommodate all the villagers who are inviting themselves, never mind the doctor and his friends. I shrug and decide that it's not my problem and I'll leave them to Aunt Shiphra.

It's the same in the other stalls, and in the end we leave the square empty-handed, watching laden donkeys and even a camel being led to our house.

Mara and I are back on water-drawing duty, although we're allowed to snatch a few pastries dipped in cream, and a bruised peach which has been rejected from the table. It's the nearest we'll get to a meal today. Again we face the clamour of questions. The only person who continues to pretend I'm not there is Imma, who passes by me on her way to one of the stalls.

By the time we're back, the sheep are no longer bleating but hanging by their hind legs from the branches of the apricot tree, blood still dripping from their slit necks into bowls beneath them as two men begin to slice expertly around them, preparing to draw off the outer skin whole. There are more women meekly following Marta and Shiphra's orders, and they've already run out of water. We can barely keep up. The vegetable patch is swimming in discarded water used for washing carrots and other vegetables, and the herb patch can no longer mask the smell from our unclean place, which is getting a lot more usage than it would normally. I suspect our bucket of flat stones used for wiping has been depleted, and so I dispatch one of the neighbour girls down to the brook to collect more and to bring back fresh fig leaves, which we'll put out when the guests arrive. She bows, takes a friend with her and they're off. I've never issued an order and been obeyed like that before.

Mara and I are wet from spilled water and sweat. We pause under a tree on our way back to the well, knowing there'll be no rest either at home or at the well itself. One thing I like about

Chris Aslan

being busy is that it doesn't really give me time to think about Father or about Eleazar. I have to admit that all this excitement is contagious and I'm pretty curious to see this doctor. I wonder how he cures people, and what he charges. I also wonder if he can cure crazy people, or if Cyria's hopes will be dashed. I've never met anyone important before, and imagine him riding into the village on a canopied camel or a pure white horse.

"Come on," says Mara, and off we go.

Back at the compound, the sheep are being noisily hacked into smaller portions by our heftiest cleaver-wielding neighbour. One of the elders has brought us an enormous water jar from the prayer house. They must have used a camel to bring it over. Even empty it takes several people to manoeuvre it into position. We pour our jars into it and they barely seem to make a difference. Even so, the water is depleted as best plates and bowls are lent and washed. Several neighbour girls boil mint tea and go around offering it to the busy workers. We also pause for a quick bowlful each. It's a good thing its summer and our vegetable patch is soaking most of the discarded water up – at least for now.

"If you're tired of carrying I can get one of the women to swap with you," says Marta, looking up from a large mound of fine mutton chunks which she and some other women are busy skewering. She looks fraught. Mara and I, by silent agreement, shake our heads. Although water-carrying is hard work, at least it's a lot less stressful than being stuck in a compound crammed with people.

On our next water delivery, Marta is crying. "They're saying we can't host here because the upper room isn't fit for use," she says.

"Who is saying?"

"Everyone. Why couldn't Malchus have come a few days earlier? We don't have enough time to get ready."

"Look," I say. "I don't know much about this doctor, but he could have requested to visit the prayer house or any number of nicer compounds. For whatever reason, he's chosen to come here; to Eleazar's house. It'll be a warm evening. He'll be fine with the

135

other important guests up on the roof, away from all this." I point at the cramped space around us, brimming with neighbours.

"How can we expect him to climb a ladder?" she says. "And there's no shade."

"I'm sure he's got legs." I give her a quick hug. She smells of stress-sweat; we could both use a wash in the brook. "Look, the sun is already losing its heat. I'm sure they'll prefer the cool of the roof to a stuffy upper room."

I lose track of how many visits to the well we make. My arms ache and I think I might have a bruise in the crook of my shoulder where I nestle the water jug. By now, the compound is filled with smoke from a long charcoal pit over which the mutton is sizzling. There's also a steaming cauldron full of sheep bones. Neighbours have lent us their best seating mats, which have been carried up the ladder by one of the stronger youths. Mara and I offer to take some of the dishes of food up to the roof so we can see if the guest area looks good enough. Mother's carpets have been laid out along with others borrowed from neighbours, topped with seating mats in rows to allow for the largest number of people possible. Cushions are propped against the low wall around the flat roof, with the largest and finest of these along the opposite wall to the ladder, in the place of honour.

I climb up on the wall and stand on tiptoe, screening my eyes against the setting sun. There are too many trees obscuring the view to the main road, so I can't tell if the doctor is on his way yet.

"Water!" I hear Marta shout from below, and we clamber down, take our jars and head back to the well.

Mara is just helping me lift my jar when we hear the sound of a procession coming up from down near the brook. "He's here," she cries, and we race back to the compound, water slopping everywhere. "They're coming," Mara announces, and there's a sudden flurry of activity, like when you poke a twig into an ants' nest.

Aunt Shiphra has given up policing who comes in and who

doesn't, and instead she and Elisheba prepare the spiced oil to pour over the head of each guest. Marta stops what she's doing for just long enough to pass me and Mara clean linen cloths and a ewer each. "There's a dipper behind you to refill the ewers," she says. "And if there's not enough water to wash the feet of all the guests, make sure you at least get the most important ones."

We form a line of welcome with Marta, Auntie Shiphra, and Elisheba first, and then me and Mara, crouched down near one of the vegetable furrows, hoping that the water from the feet-washing drains into the vegetable patch, which is starting to get pretty waterlogged.

The first guest to walk through the compound door is Halfai. I try not to roll my eyes. No one has invited him, he always shuns us, and the last time he was inside our compound was to exile my father. He's wearing his finest robe, and makes a show of bowing his head for oil and then lifting his feet for Mara to pour water over them and his sandals. He leaves his wet sandals at the foot of the ladder, and they're soon surrounded by so many that Sholum is dispatched to stack them in piles.

I'm squatting, trying to keep the hem of my tunic from getting too muddy as we attempt to wash the feet of each guest. Although Halfai slipped through, someone has had the good sense to keep the villagers outside and to let the doctor and his entourage through first. It's hard to see much at foot level, but I keep looking out for Malchus or Eleazar or Yokkan. I spot Malchus first. He tries to stop me from washing his feet, but I won't have it. Holding the heel of his foot and seeing the unblemished skin makes his cure even more real.

"Which one's the doctor?" I ask. "And why wasn't he first to enter?"

"He's just coming in now." Malchus points vaguely at the compound door. "He was probably stopped by people outside wanting to receive his blessing or to be cured."

I look up and my eyes are drawn to a handsome man with

piercing green eyes, a sandy beard and light skin, and an aura about him that just makes me want to listen to anything he has to say. He's wearing a richly embroidered robe and he approaches me, lifting up his heel. I take extra care as I wash his feet. "You are most welcome to our home," I say. "Thank you for all you've done."

He doesn't pay me much attention, more amused at having to climb a ladder to get to the banquet. I still can't see Eleazar or Yokkan, who will probably come in after their elders.

Another foot is presented and I focus on washing. By now my linen cloth is soaked and a little grubby from where it dragged in the mud for a moment. A strand of hair has escaped my headscarf and plastered itself to my forehead. I try to blow it away but it won't budge.

"Here," says a voice, and a hand gently brushes it away. I nod in gratitude and then he presents his heel and I hurry, washing one foot and then the other – not that my grubby cloth has done much more than muddy the dust on his feet.

"Master, this is my cousin, Eleazar's sister," says another voice above me, and I almost lose my balance when I realize that it's Yokkan speaking. His beard is full and he's completely lost all his boyishness. I clamber to my feet and hug him. Then Eleazar is there beside him. I realize that I'm crying as I take in the lean young man he's become, taller than Father but with the same expression. I thought I'd slap him or ignore him, but seeing so much of Father in him, I can't stop weeping as we embrace.

The other man, whose feet I've just hastily washed, smiles, his kind eyes shining with tears. He's weather-worn, with marked laughter lines and rough, worker's hands. He clasps Eleazar around the neck with one of them and then kisses him tenderly on the forehead. "This is what courage is," he says quietly to Eleazar, who reddens. "Thank you for returning."

"You're him," I say with mounting horror, clutching my dirty linen cloth in hand and looking absently at the ladder up which

138

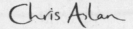

the man I thought was the doctor climbed a while back. "Wait, let me get a fresh cloth. I didn't do it properly. Please, I need to do your feet again."

"Thank you – my feet are fine," the man smiles, and Eleazar leads him to the ladder. I have no time to think because more feet are presented to me and the muddy ground is getting treacherously slippery and harder to squat in.

Thankfully, most of the villagers who follow after the guests take one look at the mud slough and protest that they've already washed their feet just before coming. There is barely room to move inside the compound, and the vegetable patch is being trampled. Some of them are up to their ankles in its mud. There's standing room only, except for the youths who've perched themselves up in the branches of the tree and along the compound mud walls.

"Get back," Marta shouts, as someone is pushed and steps onto one of the bowls of strained yogurt and mint, flipping the contents everywhere. She's near breaking point. I grab two of the other bowls in similarly precarious situations, and hold them over my head as I push my way through the crowd. I manage to balance one bowl in the crook of my arm, giving me a free hand to climb the ladder. This whole situation is ridiculous; there are well over a hundred people crammed into our compound. What was Malchus thinking?

However, up on the roof there seems to be more order. The sun is now a red semi-orb in the west and there's a breeze. Halfai, I notice, has seated himself at the right hand of the doctor. I'm glad to see that someone has ushered the doctor to the place of honour. Something tells me that he wouldn't have sat there otherwise. The ladder wobbles. I look down to see Sholum and Little Marta trying to keep their balance and not lose any of the contents of their bowls. They both look tired and overwhelmed.

"Go and place them on the floor cloth in front of the doctor, over there," I say, once they make it to the top. They look at me panic-stricken as they still hate being visible in crowds. Elisheba told me they've been that way since the stoning. "It'll be fine," I whisper with a smile. "Go on."

"Thank you," says the doctor, as they lay the bowls before him. They look up briefly and bow. "Come, girls, have a rest. Come and sit by me. You look exhausted." They look to me for advice, and I shrug helplessly. The doctor asks Halfai to make space and he is shunted along so that the girls can squeeze in. Halfai tries to suppress his disapproval, and I can't help smiling.

"Rest for a moment," someone whispers and I see that it's Malchus. He's sitting in one of the less honourable positions near the ladder, even though he paid for this whole feast. I clamber along the wall until I'm above him. I've always been a good climber.

"You should be up there, sitting with the doctor," I say. Malchus just smiles and seems content where he is. "Here," I pass him the bowls and he places them on the floor cloth laid out before them which, I have to say, looks pretty impressive. Each floor cloth is covered with flaky butter-rich flatbreads, pastries filled with dried fruit, nuts, and date syrup, bowls of curd, cheeses, strained yogurt with herbs, strained yogurt with honey and pomegranate molasses, platters of fresh bitter herbs and vegetables, and mounds of olives and peaches, grapes, and fresh figs. One of the neighbour boys picks his way between the rows, cupping a beeswax taper in his hand and lighting the lamps. Everything dances in the light of more lamps than I've ever seen. Most of our neighbours will be going to bed in the dark tonight. I look around and spot Eleazar and Yokkan sitting in the corner near the man I originally thought was the doctor.

I turn from this magical scene because there's a commotion below. I look down from my vantage point and see Cyria elbowing her way through the crowd, making for the ladder. I look for Crazy Mariam, but Cyria seems to be alone. She clambers up the ladder, breathing heavily. "Which one is him?" she asks, and people point towards the doctor. She pauses for a moment, and then approaches. It's not easy, as she has to step over people, and at least one bowl of honey gets knocked over in the process.

Halfai glowers and seems about to get up and shoo her away, but then the doctor sees her and gets to his feet. "Welcome," he says, in a way that makes it sound as if she was the honoured guest.

"Master," says Cyria. "I'm sorry to interrupt you. I won't keep you long. I've heard about your great deeds and dreamt for so long of taking my daughter to you, but I knew she wouldn't manage the long journey, and now you're here." She pauses for breath and then her face crumples. "My Mariam," she says in a high-pitched wail, and then swallows and tries to compose herself. "Please, she's very sick, and I have a cow. She's a joy to me, good-tempered, and generous with her milk." There's a titter from one of the guests. "I will happily give her to you if you could just come and see my daughter. It would only take a few moments."

"Come," says Halfai, taking control. How could he resist? "Let the teacher rest and eat. Don't bother him any further. Perhaps, if he has time, he can see you tomorrow."

"What would you have me do for your daughter?" asks the doctor, as if it wasn't clear already.

"I just want you to make her better," says Cyria, her face knotted with an expression between hope and despair.

"And do you think I can?"

"Yes."

"Then go to her," he says. She pauses for a moment, unsure if he's helped her or dismissed her. "Keep her at home tomorrow," the doctor adds. "Let her get used to you."

Cyria stumbles backwards and then hurries down the ladder. I lean back over the wall and watch as she and some of her neighbours push their way to the door and run down the darkening street. The ladder wobbles as someone else attempts to climb it in a hurry. It's Shoshanna's neighbour, Ide. She struggles to haul herself up, her club foot useless when it comes to ladders.

I've never seen Ide as anything more than an unpleasant gossip. Now I watch her as people stare. She's frightened, but something beyond fear motivates her. Her limp seems more pronounced as she clumsily makes her way forward, stepping on people's feet and spilling things.

"I've heard that you can make people well – even people who have been deformed since birth. Please, can you help me?" She steps closer and lifts her tunic hem a little, presenting her club foot to the doctor.

"Do you believe I can?" he asks, and she pauses and then nods. He leans forward and places his hand on her clawed foot and then prays, or at least I think he's praying, but he speaks to God as Father. She cries out and I wonder if he's hurt her. There's a moment of silence as she stares down at her foot and then she yells. It's a cry of joy, I think, but then she starts weeping and I'm not sure what's happened exactly, until she starts jumping.

"It works, it works! My foot works!" she cries, and there are gasps from the guests on the roof.

"What's happened?" someone cries from down below.

"He's just cured Ide of her club foot. It's completely restored," I call back and the whole compound erupts.

Ide falls at the doctor's feet weeping and thanking him, and asking how much she should pay. He just laughs. She hurries over to the ladder. "Look!" she shouts, lifting up her foot. "He cured me! He did it!" She starts climbing down the ladder in a way that would have been impossible just moments before, but her feet never reach the ground. Instead the villagers lift her up and carry her along over their heads, everyone reaching out to touch the foot that has been restored. "I'm cured, I'm cured!" I hear Ide shout above the crowd. We've never seen anything like this. I turn back in wonder. There's nothing remarkable about the doctor's appearance. He doesn't even have any medicines with him. How does he do it? The guests are laughing in joy and wonder, although many of the followers seem completely unsurprised and are already tucking into the feast.

Who is this man?

Everyone seems so happy. Everyone, that is, except Halfai.

Chapter Ten

It's dark now, and time for the lamps to be trimmed and refilled. One of the neighbours passes up a jar of oil and I pick my way amongst the guests, pouring a little into each lamp. Little Marta and Sholum have curled up together beside the doctor, fast asleep. Apart from them, I'm the only girl up here. No one pays me any attention, though, as they're all listening to the doctor speak, utterly transfixed. I can see now why Malchus refers to him as the teacher. I've never heard anyone who can talk like this.

When he first starts to speak of God, I lose interest and collect empty plates, which we'll need again for the meat course, still sizzling over the charcoal pit down below. I can't help listening, though, and by the time I've collected a stack, he's caught my interest and I'm reluctant to climb down the ladder. I manage to get down without dropping anything and pass the plates to one of the neighbours below.

"Has he cured anyone else?" she asks eagerly.

"No, he's just talking."

Many of the villagers have left now that the drama is over. I can hear the sounds of celebration drifting over from my old street, and I assume Ide is throwing a party. Most of those remaining here are neighbours and relatives, helping. Some are washing plates and the water is running low.

"Miri," Marta calls. "Could you go down to the well?" I find her sprinkling chopped bitter herbs over the chunks of mutton.

"That's all I've been doing all day. Can't you get someone else to do it?"

"What, and I've been sitting around fanning myself and feeding myself grapes?" Marta snaps. "Listen, I haven't got time for this."

"I'll go soon; just let me listen to the teacher for a little bit. Really, Marta, you should come up."

"Oof!" she says, shaking her head in despair, which I decide to interpret as grudging permission.

"Tell me, what are the main crops in your village? Do you have vineyards?" the teacher is asking the guests as I perch myself up on the flat roof wall.

"Olives," I say. I'd almost forgotten he was speaking to everyone, as it feels as if he's speaking just to me. Halfai, Eleazar and one or two other guests shoot me disapproving looks; a girl should know her place. Malchus looks up at me and smiles mischievously.

"Excellent," says the teacher, picking up an olive from the floor cloth and holding it out for us all to see. "A landowner with a huge olive grove must harvest his olives. Early one morning he goes down to the market to find day labourers to hire." I've heard about day labourers, although no one in our village has enough land to need them.

Malchus beckons me and I lean over towards him. "This story helped me so much. Pay attention," he whispers.

"He offers a generous day-pay to anyone willing to come and harvest his olives, and then leads the labourers to his grove and they climb the trees and begin to beat them. They work hard, and he supplies them with sacks for the olives and water for their thirst as the day hots up. Then he returns to the market to buy food for the labourers and he sees more men waiting around, hoping to find work that day. 'Come,' he says. 'You can also work for me for the rest of the day and I promise to pay you what is right.' They follow him and join the harvest. The grove-owner returns again to the market to collect more day labourers, first during the afternoon and then as the sun begins to go down."

I'm not sure how a story about olive harvesting has helped Malchus, but I can't help being drawn in.

"At sunset, the last sack is filled and the labourers gather around the grove-owner to collect their wages. He pays those who came last, first. They each receive the generous day-pay; it's the same amount as promised to those who have been working all day, and they leave amazed at his generosity. The other labourers who've worked all morning see this generosity and now they expect to get paid more. However, as each labourer comes forward, all receive the same day-pay. 'This is unfair,' they grumble. 'We've worked hard all day, enduring the noonday heat. We should get paid more.'

"'But didn't you yourselves thank me this morning for offering a generous day-pay?' says the grove-owner. 'Have I paid you less than I promised? What's it to you if I choose to be even more generous with these others?'

"And so the last will be first."

The teacher sits back and pops the olive into his mouth.

"Is that the end?" I whisper to Malchus. I don't understand the story, or why the teacher is telling it to us.

"Teacher, what does the story mean?" I ask. There's a ripple of muttering that a girl would brazenly speak out amongst older men. I studiously avoid eye contact with Halfai or Eleazar, focusing only on the teacher.

"What do you think it means?" he asks me back. There's a further flurry of disapproval.

"I – I don't know." I suddenly feel very self-conscious. "But isn't he being unfair? I'd be upset if I was one of the labourers."

"Which labourer?" the teacher asks, with a smile. "What if

you'd been waiting all day hoping for work, wondering if you'd be able to afford an evening meal, and then you got paid a generous day-pay for just an hour of labour?"

I smile shyly. I hadn't thought of that. He continues to tell us stories about everyday life, but from each of them he pulls out something important. I glance around and notice that Eleazar is missing. Then I hear a hiss from the top of the ladder. It's Marta with a meat plate. A few rungs down I see Eleazar glowering up at me. I go to take the plate from Marta and start serving, but she doesn't let go of it.

"Get down there," she whispers fiercely. "El says you've been bothering the doctor with questions. Leave the learning to the men."

"I only asked one question," I whisper back. "Here, just pass the plates up and I'll hand them out."

"No," Marta hisses back. "El's barely been home an evening and already you've embarrassed him in front of his master. Just get downstairs and keep out of the way."

A few guests give us silencing looks as we both tug at the plate of skewered mutton. Then the teacher clears his throat. He's looking at us. "And this is?"

Marta lets go of the plate and I hurry over to lay it at the teacher's feet. "This is my sister, Marta," I say. "She's the one who has prepared the feast for us."

"Thank you, Marta. You've been an excellent host, and at such short notice. It's an honour to enjoy your hospitality. Come, please join us. You must be hungry."

"But there's still the meat course," says Marta, frozen. Everyone is looking at her and she's obviously close to tears. "I need Mariam to help me. She's just left me to do everything. I'm sorry she's been bothering you. Please tell her to come and help me."

The teacher gets up, comes over to Marta and puts a hand on her shoulder, at which point she begins to weep. "Marta," he says with such gentleness it makes her look up at him as if the rest of

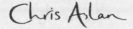

us no longer exist. "You've been so busy downstairs preparing this wonderful feast, but that's not why I came here. Look, your sister has chosen the better way; let's not take it away from her. Come. Let's eat together."

He leads her over to the place of honour and she sits reluctantly beside her sleeping apprentices. Then he offers her the meat plate, insisting that she take the first bite. Halfai, glowering, is displaced yet again.

Although we've spent the whole day preparing food for the doctor, I feel as if he's the one feeding us. Looking at the dark expression on Halfai's face in the flickering lamplight, beside the serene faces of the sleeping apprentices, I'm starting to understand the story of the olive grove. The last will be first.

I wake, cold and cramped, and don't know where I am. I try to move but someone's head rests heavily on my leg. I look around and my eyes adjust to the darkness, and then I notice a lighter square of stars and the beginning of dawn. I gently ease Marta's head off my leg and pull myself up. The apprentices are curled together with their heads resting on Marta's belly like two suckling kittens. There's straw in my hair, and I'm not sure why, until I realize that we've made a nest for ourselves in the stable. Our donkey is lying next to us, his legs daintily folded beneath him. Apart from the smell of straw and donkey, there's still a smoky tang in the air from the mutton, mingled with less pleasant smells, such as the overflowing unclean place and many unwashed people in close proximity. I stretch my neck and wander outside pulling straw from my hair, wondering what woke me up. I see two figures talking quietly under the apricot tree.

One of them has their back to me and the other is Malchus. He seems about to leave. I adjust my headscarf and go over to him. "Are you leaving?" I ask, and both men turn round. The other is the teacher.

"I'm going to the colony. If I leave now, the lepers will have

147

time to walk to the main road before the teacher moves on. He can cure them," says Malchus.

I nod. "And why are you leaving?" I ask, turning to the teacher. I always end up sounding far too direct and rude when I speak to him, and I immediately colour. "Sorry. I mean, we would love for you to stay."

"And put your poor sister through another day of hosting us all?" he says, with a grin. "There really are a lot of us."

"I don't know how you manage being with people all day every day," I say. I don't seem able to shut up.

He widens his eyes in an expression that says, "I know exactly what you mean." Then he says, "Actually, perhaps you could help me. I have a request."

"Would you like some more mutton?" I ask. I can't say anything right.

"No; just some peace and quiet. Tell me, where could I go to just be alone to think and pray?"

I grin. "In our village? There aren't many places. How about our land? We own a grove up the hill. It's wonderfully quiet there, especially at this time of year."

"Could you take me?"

I glance at Malchus. I'm not sure if it's appropriate for me to be alone with an unmarried man, but Malchus just looks at me as if I've been given a great honour. So I step over Auntie Shiphra and several neighbours who are asleep in the kitchen area, and off we go.

For a while we walk in silence. I love this time of the morning, as the olive trees no longer loom threateningly in the dark, but gradually lighten and will soon offer shade from the rising sun. "I haven't been to our grove for a while. I've been meaning to check on the saplings I helped Father plant. He knew every tree as if it was a friend."

"I've heard about your father from Malchus," the teacher says. I notice that it wasn't from Eleazar. "I wish I could have met him."

Chris Aslan

"I wish you could have, too," I say, and my eyes suddenly blur with tears. I feel embarrassed, but the teacher doesn't seem to mind; we just continue walking. "He tried to find you. He wanted you to cure him, too, but he didn't make it."

"I'm so sorry," he says.

"So am I."

We reach the grove and the teacher looks around. "It'll be harvest time in a few months," he says. "Who will help you?"

"I don't know," I say. It's something I've been thinking about a lot. "We could really do with some of those day labourers you talked about last night."

We both smile. He chooses a tree, takes off his linen shawl and lays it down to sit on. My smile fades. He looks up questioningly. "Do you mind if I stay here to pray?"

"Please, make yourself at home," I say. He's chosen the exact place where Ishmael raped me. "But wouldn't you prefer the shade of a different tree?"

"Is there something wrong with this one?" he asks. Of course, I can't say anything – I just shake my head. I feel his gaze on me.

Then he starts to pray for me. At first I don't realize he's praying and look around because he's talking to his father, but there's no one else here. He hasn't assumed the correct position for praying and he's not using the holy language we're supposed to pray in. All I know is that I'm flooded with a sense of peace and calm. I realize, suddenly, that whenever I pass this tree from now on, I won't remember the rape – I'll remember this moment. I'm crying, but I'm not sad. His words are just for me.

Back at the compound, Marta is relieved to see me. "Everyone's disappearing. Malchus is gone, too, and so is the doctor."

I tell her that the teacher wants to spend some time alone. Looking at Marta, I suspect he's not the only one. "And Malchus went to the colony to organize the lepers. He's leading them all to the main road so that the doctor can cure them."

149

"But what if he gets reinfected?" says Marta.

I shrug. "I suppose he'll just get cured again." Marta's cheeks look hollowed out. "They're leaving today." I put an arm around her. "I'm sorry that I upset you yesterday."

"No, the doctor was right," she says. "His words were so, so rich. I feel like I've swallowed a sheep without chewing. Once everything quietens down and I'm back at my loom, I'm going to mull over everything he said and digest it properly. I'm so glad I got to hear him and didn't just stay in the kitchen."

"Me too. Where are El and Yokkan?"

"They're still up on the roof asleep with some of the other guests. Come, help me prepare breakfast, and we could do with some more water."

The day grows steadily more chaotic. Up on the roof, the guests are fed on plentiful leftovers from last night, and then Eleazar and Yokkan suggest a trip to the brook to bathe, as the teacher still hasn't returned. We manage to clear up the roof, but soon we're busy providing leftovers for a growing number of sick who have come to our home from the smaller villages nearby. Word has spread. There's an old woman almost doubled over with a hunched back, a young shepherd from our own village with a severe squint, a pretty little girl with a disfiguring skin rash down one side of her face, and a boy of around twelve who has been put in an extra robe, worn the wrong way round with the sleeves tied behind him to keep his arms away from his face, which he seems desperate to claw.

These sick people are the reason most of the bystanders from our village have gathered – hoping to see a spectacular curing, but also not wanting to get too close, lest they themselves be infected with misfortune. There's a commotion as the doctor is spotted trudging down from the olive hills.

Aunt Shiphra rolls up her tunic sleeves and marches outside. "Let him through," she barks. "He hasn't eaten anything yet. Let him have some breakfast and then he'll see you." She's reassuringly formidable and holds the crowd back to let the teacher past. He rewards her with a grateful smile, and then Marta hurries him to the ladder. He'll have the roof almost to himself and we've plumped the cushions and laid out his own private feast. Marta, apparently, was watching him as he taught last night, observing whatever he seemed to pick at most from all the plates before him, and now we've assembled his favourites. Mara even managed to rig up a few poles and some sacking to provide shade.

He doesn't make the ladder. "Master," a tearful woman pleads. "Please, it's my son. He's full of devils. They make him do terrible things to himself." As if he's following her cue, the boy tied in the robe falls to the ground, shrieking and writhing about, savagely kicking the squinting shepherd. The villagers crowd in to watch the spectacle, and our compound wall is swiftly lined with youths. I'm being jostled dangerously close to the flailing boy and manage to dash past him and up a few rungs of the ladder.

"Get out!" the teacher commands, and the boy gives an ear-piercing scream, arching his back as his mother flutters helplessly around him, and then he collapses. I'm not the only one to gasp.

"Is he dead?" a few people ask.

The teacher kneels down and unties the sleeves of the robe, gently tugging them loose. The boy opens his eyes and looks up at him. "Thank you," he says.

"No," says the mother, eyes wide. "It's not possible. He's never spoken a word before."

"Help him up," says the teacher.

Together they help the boy to his feet. "Thank you," he says again to the teacher, and then turns to the woman and says, "Thank you, Mother." For a moment she just looks at him, as if winded.

"Oh, my boy," she gasps, clasping him to her. "Oh, my precious boy." They weep together.

I'm crying now, as are some of the others around me; even some of the youths up on the wall. Other people are cheering, and one woman starts to ululate in celebration. There's no time to stop and remind ourselves that what the teacher is doing isn't possible.

We watch in amazement as he cures each of them. Amongst the crowd I see Ishmael with his arm round Imma's shoulders. Next to them are Rivka and Shoshanna. I feel a twinge of jealousy for a moment, but then I see their expressions of wonder and I'm glad that their curiosity to even enter our courtyard was stronger than their disdain of me.

I see Eleazar and the other guests come up the street but there's no way they'll get past the crowd, which keeps encroaching, and the teacher has to keep backing up until he actually climbs a few rungs of the ladder. I scamper up to the roof to give him space as he perches himself on the highest rung and begins to teach.

The crowd grows quiet. Everyone wants to hear what he has to say. I notice Marta down below, making faces at me. It takes me a moment to understand what she's trying to communicate, and I nod. I take one of the fresh flatbreads from the carefully laid food cloth and heap up a plate of boiled eggs, olives, strained yogurt with herbs, and honey yogurt, passing it to him to graze as he speaks. He won't starve.

We lose track of time and the teacher stops only when we hear the distinct clanging of approaching bells. People look at each other. They know the sound but they can't work out why we're hearing it inside the village. Then we hear the voices: "Unclean, unclean."

The crowd protests and a few look around them for stones to throw. Why are these lepers breaking the law and entering the village? Fear of contagion is stronger than curiosity and the crowd jostles and pushes, clearing the way from the well to our compound. Inside the compound, people shrink back. I fear that my trampled vegetable patch will never recover. Leading the lepers is Malchus. In his arms is a ragged bundle. I realize that he's carrying one of the lepers.

Malchus steps through the compound doorway but the lepers pause, unsure.

Chris Aslan

"Come," says Marta, stepping forward. "Come in. You're welcome here."

The teacher climbs down the ladder. There are around eight of them. Malchus lays down the woman in his arms. She's the first one the teacher touches. He actually touches her. People look at each other in shock.

"Auntie, be well," he says. He stretches out his hand and she takes it. Then he helps her to her feet. She pulls away the rags that cover her mouth and begins to explore herself for signs of the disease. It's hard for any of us to tell if she's been cured or not, as she's pitifully gaunt. However, I look again and she seems to be growing healthier before our very eyes. "Marta," says the teacher, and Marta nods, fetching some food for the woman to eat. The crowd is too gripped to cheer, and we watch as the teacher touches each of the lepers and cures them. It's as if his wholeness, his wellness, is more contagious; more powerful.

"Now show yourselves to your holy man and give thanks to God," says the teacher. Malchus has an enormous grin on his face as his eyes shine with tears and he grabs the teacher in a fierce embrace. The lepers, or ex-lepers, still seem in shock, staring at one another, and touching each other's skin in wonder. Then one of the leper women starts to laugh and grabs Mara, drawing her into a little jig. Mara is frozen for a moment, every instinct telling her to shrink back. She peers closer and it's clear that this woman has been cured. Mara laughs shyly and then enters into the spirit of things, and they start to dance together.

What is happening? The laws of our village are ripping at the seams as lepers mingle with villagers, who in their joy embrace them. Both throw their hands in the air thanking God. I see one of my neighbours disappear into her compound and come out with several robes, which she gives to the most ragged of the lepers, and then another neighbour does likewise. I didn't realize it was possible to laugh and cry at the same time. I feel so overwhelmed.

How has this one man managed to change the lives not just of the sick, but of all of us? Our village will never be the same again. A thought suddenly pierces my heart. What if Father had stayed in the colony? If he'd conserved his strength would he be here now, laughing and healthy, joining in the celebration?

The well-dressed guest I'd mistaken for the doctor yesterday climbs up on the wall and manages to get the teacher's attention. It seems it's time for them to leave.

The teacher looks back up at me. "Thank you for breakfast, Mariam," he says. "I'm glad you're my apprentice."

I can't believe that he's given me this honour, and I smile through my tears as the crowd sweeps him out of our compound and down the street. I stay behind helping Marta to put together a sack of food that will travel well. We run after the crowd, which is at the well, and follow until we go past the brook and the stoning spot. The teacher stops and calls for Marta and me. I think it's because he wants the sack of food. He doesn't even notice it. Instead, he thanks us both for opening our home to him, and then he embraces us. We're not even related or married. This man really doesn't know the rules of our village, but no one seems to mind.

"Eleazar, Yokkan." He calls them forward. I've barely had time to think about them with everything that's gone on. "I want you to stay."

"What?" says Eleazar.

"But we're your apprentices," says Yokkan. "Where you go, we go."

"A true apprentice obeys his master's command," says the teacher. He clasps Eleazar's neck in his hand and leans forward so their foreheads touch. It's an intimate gesture. "I promise I will come back to you," the teacher says softly. "But there's work I have for you here in the village."

"What work?" Eleazar sounds uncertain.

"You're good at going. Now I want you to learn to stay. Your sisters will teach you," he adds, with a smile in our direction.

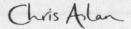

Chris Aslan

"And the harvest will be ripe soon." I think he means our olives. "Yokkan, you too."

Yokkan nods. He's never been that obedient with anyone. "But can we walk with you halfway to the capital?"

The teacher agrees.

"Where's Malchus?" says Marta. We ask around but apparently he's helping the healed lepers with something. "He didn't say goodbye," she whispers sadly.

We watch as the teacher and his apprentices and many of the young men from the village walk along the main road, a small dust cloud following in their wake.

"There you are."

We turn around and see Malchus with some others; they're all wet. I have to look twice before I recognize them as the former lepers. Dressed in clean clothes and freshly bathed from the brook, they're barely recognizable.

Marta lights up in the way she used to with Annas. "We thought you'd gone," she says.

"How could I leave without thanking you both and all of your neighbours and relatives for hosting us so wonderfully? I'm truly grateful."

"Really, it was nothing," says Marta, beaming, and I snort, giving her a playful shove. "Well, it did feel a little overwhelming," she adds.

"Next time, I'll serve you. I promise," he says. We look puzzled. "I'm coming back to help you harvest the olives," he says. "It's the teacher's wish." With a parting grin, he and the other cured lepers are off.

We walk back through the village. People smile and nod to us in greeting. It seems that our social standing has been transformed almost as much as the lepers'. We pause at the well, where a group of women are eagerly gathered around a stranger, asking her questions. I peer closer and realize that it's Crazy Mariam.

She's shy, but articulate and unexpectedly pretty. I think of the

155

jokes I've heard people make about her over the years, and the times we've mocked her. I remember one time, as girls, we threw stones at her when she came too close because we were worried she would attack us, even though she just wanted to play with us.

"Mariam," I say, taking one of her hands in mine. "It's so good to see you like this." We both smile awkwardly at each other. "Could you ask your mother for me if she's free the day after tomorrow? We'd like to invite you both to our home."

She smiles earnestly. "Where do you live?"

"Our home is where the teacher stayed," I say. She'll remember that. We all will.

Returning to our home, we're faced with a scene of utter ruin. My vegetable patch is now a refuse pond. Looking closer, someone's sandal bobs semi-submerged amongst mutton bones and vegetable peelings. There are borrowed pots, plates, lamps, and seating mats everywhere.

"I know what you're like," I say to Marta with a sigh. "You won't be able to rest until everything is clean and put away. I'll fetch water."

We spend the rest of the day clearing up. Aunt Shiphra and Mara come to help us, even though they're as exhausted as we are. Still, it's a pleasant kind of exhaustion, and every now and then one of us will say, "Could you believe it when – " and then recount one of the many recent marvels.

Borrowed bowls and plates are returned heaped with leftovers. I'm tasked with carrying clay lamps up and down the street, trying to ensure that everyone gets their own lamp back. Then I do the same with the seating mats. At least we don't have to worry about preparing meals today or for the next few days, as we can easily subsist on all the leftovers.

As it turns out, we even end up with hot date cakes. Ide brings them round in the afternoon. She dances in, pinches my cheeks, and then plants a large kiss on my forehead. I try not to pull away. "God bless you," she says to me. "God bless you for bringing the

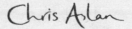

doctor to us." I don't try to correct her – she's too busy twirling, showing off her restored foot. She laughs and leaves. We can't help smiling.

"I'm glad Ide is the subject of so much village gossip right now," I say. "But gossip about something good, and not someone else's misfortune."

I make several more trips to the well, and most of the water I bring back is used to scrub the unclean place, which is in a state best left undescribed. Finally, as the sun sets, Marta straightens her back, surveys the compound, and pronounces it clean. We've just sat down when Eleazar and Yokkan return. Yokkan, Mara, and Shiphra head back to their own compound.

For a moment we feel awkward. When we met yesterday it was in the midst of all the drama of the feast and the curing. Now it's just the three of us and at first none of us speak, and then we interrupt each other.

Marta sits Eleazar down and boils water for mint tea. I lay out some of the leftover food and date cakes, as we might as well have our evening meal now. Eleazar just looks pensive. Once we're all seated, he speaks.

"I was talking with Yokkan on the way back about what the teacher said; what he commanded us." He pauses and Marta is wise enough not to fill the silence with words. "Neither of us wanted to stay here. Being his apprentices has been a life-changing adventure. You wouldn't believe some of the things we've seen, even after what you've seen him do." He sighs. "But he's right. We ran away. Miri, I knew that you'd be fine in your new home…" I realize at this point that we never told Eleazar the real reason I was marrying Ishmael, and that he doesn't know yet that I'm divorced. "But Marta, how could I have just abandoned you to living alone? I failed you, just like I failed Father."

Marta puts a hand on his knee. I just listen. I've never seen Eleazar apologize before, but I'm not sure I'm ready to forgive him just yet. "Now I'm here again, and I want to live right. I was

157

stupid before and thought that living right meant following all the old laws. The teacher has changed everything. Being with him changes people. I've changed." He holds Marta's gaze. "I'm so sorry. I want to make it right between us." He looks at me, too, when he says that.

I want to tell him that it's too late. I want him to know that all the suffering he's caused can't just be cancelled with a few words. He's not even crying, even though Marta is freely weeping now. Why shouldn't he suffer? Anger, like an old friend, stirs in my belly. Then I think about the lepers and Not-Crazy Mariam and all the other people no one had hope for, and I think about how their lives have just changed beyond recognition in the space of one day, all because the teacher came to our village.

"I still feel really angry towards you," I say evenly to my brother. "And I'm not ready to trust you, or even forgive you. But I am ready to try."

"Come here," says Marta, and grabs us both in an uncomfortable embrace. Both Eleazar and I reach an arm around her, but we're not ready to embrace each other just yet.

Chapter Eleven

My mother was known for her carpet-weaving, but she was also good with the needle. As children, our robes and tunics constantly got torn, but she could mend the tear with tiny stitches that never rucked or pulled at the cloth, so that the tear was almost invisible. However, when it came to large rips or rents she dispensed with this method. Instead, she transformed the rip into a feature, using her brightest threads and adding a little embroidery around the tear. Eleazar had a brown-coloured robe covered in a random pattern with such details, each embroidered rip telling a story of his various scrapes with tree branches or thorn bushes.

Now, it's the same with me and Eleazar. We don't pretend that our relationship isn't torn and can be mended to look like new, but we are both making an effort to stitch it back together. The other day, Eleazar offered to peel carrots as we prepared for supper. "What? I'm actually quite good with a knife," he said, slicing the skin off the carrot as we stared at him in astonishment. He's never helped before. Then, yesterday, after Crazy Mariam and Cyria had left, he said, "You've got to think of a different name for her. What about Beautiful Mariam?"

"Hmm. And what does that make me?" I asked, cuffing him round the head. We both laughed, and then suddenly felt self-conscious and became more reserved again. Something that's helping mend the tear is that we talk.

Eleazar wanted to know why I'd run away from such a good man as Ishmael. Marta could see me getting upset by the question. "Miri," she said. "Could you fetch water? I'll explain."

When I came back, Eleazar looked shaken. It seemed as though he was about to say something but couldn't find the right words. Instead he took the water jug from me and then he hugged me, fiercely and protectively.

"The teacher taught us not to seek revenge but to forgive," he whispered. "Otherwise I'd kill him for dishonouring you like that, Miri. I'm sorry I failed you."

We asked Eleazar about his time with the insurgents. He said he didn't want to talk about it and that he still felt shame and remorse over some of the things they did. The teacher had talked to him about new life, and he didn't want to dwell on his old one. He did mention that the leader of their faction – the man I thought was the doctor – was called Shimon, like Father. When Shimon heard the teacher speak, he realized that this man had more power than any fighter. Most of the other insurgents left and started a new group, but Shimon, Eleazar, Yokkan and a few others became the teacher's apprentices.

I've noticed a change in both boys, and not just physically. Yokkan will never be a great talker, but whereas before he seemed sullen, now he just seems thoughtful. Without telling anyone, he spent the first day after the teacher had gone speaking to the three different carpenters in our village and learning about each of their skills. Two focus on buildings – mainly roof beams – but one has a lathe and produces rolling pins, chopping boards, wooden cradles, and simple shelves. Although Yokkan is too old, he asked the master carpenter to take him on as an apprentice, and Aunt Shiphra was given a glowing report over how hard-working and diligent he is. Yokkan's not earning yet – and anyway, Aunt Shiphra and Mara make ends meet with their orchard and the soap, balms, and lotions they make – but he's trying.

So, Yokkan is learning a trade, but what about my brother? With an extra mouth to feed, and most of the olive harvest left to rot last year, money is tight, and we discuss work options with Eleazar.

I tell him about the carpet business and last year's spoiled harvest. "That's my fault," he says. "If I hadn't run away, and wasn't so busy learning the law, I could have finished the harvest and brined the olives. I'm sorry."

"It's in the past now," says Marta, patting his knee. "And we still have the jar."

"Of olives?" Eleazar looks confused and we remember that he doesn't know. I go to Mother's chest and bring it out. We let Eleazar hold it in the afternoon sunlight so it glints and flashes. He puts his nose to it, but the alabaster locks the scent inside.

"I love to imagine what pure spikenard actually smells like," I say. "This jar has travelled further than any of us could ever dream."

"How did Father come by it?" Eleazar asks.

I'm about to lie – I can do it without thinking – but instead, I tell my siblings what really happened. They listen in silence and remain that way after I stop speaking.

"I don't ever want to sell it," says Marta, after a while. "Think how much this gift cost Father."

We're quiet again until Eleazar says quietly, "I know what I want to be. How I want to spend my days." We look to him expectantly. "I want to be a holy man."

"What? Like Halfai?" I'm incredulous.

"No, not like Halfai at all. Like the teacher. I want to tell other people what he taught us. They need to know."

And I have to admit, he's very good at it. Two evenings ago he invited his old friends to our home, even though our compound is still known by everyone as the leper's home. Marta and I served them. They wanted to hear all about his time with the insurgents, and whether he'd killed any Westerners. Instead, he spent most of the evening telling them about the teacher. Marta and I squatted out of the lamplight and listened just as avidly. He speaks well. He'd make a good holy man.

As for Halfai, he's been pretty quiet since the teacher was here. He seems diminished by the success of others, and all people talk about now is the teacher. He's also been busy with the wedding. Ishmael and Imma are now married. Obviously we weren't invited, but I hope Imma will be happy. Yesterday I bumped into my old neighbour, Ide, who told me about it. She also mentioned that Halfai had asked her to stop spreading stories about how she was cured.

"I just looked at him and said, 'But think of all the other people out there who need curing. How will they know about the doctor if I don't tell everyone what he's done for me?' He just told me again to keep my mouth shut."

The day after we show Eleazar the jar, he and Yokkan have a meeting with Halfai and the elders at the prayer house. It's hard to believe how little time has passed since the teacher was here, and yet so much has changed. Marta is weaving with the apprentices, while I'm trying to coax life and order back into my soggy vegetable patch. As I work, I can't help feeling anxious about this meeting. I remember what Eleazar was like when he was Halfai's apprentice, and I'd hate to see him revert to that again.

Marta has embarked on a more complex carpet design, as she thinks the apprentices need the challenge. They're all completely engrossed so, once I've finished tending the vegetable patch, I fetch water and then make a start with supper. That's what I'm doing when Yokkan and Eleazar burst in.

"He's shunned us," says Yokkan, who spits for good measure.

"He's told the elders that no one is to greet us in the street, sell to us, speak to us, or invite us into their homes," adds Eleazar. They're both fuming.

Marta glances at the apprentices, apparently unsure if she wants them to hear more, but then comes over to the kitchen area. "What happened?" She beckons them to sit down and I pour mint tea.

"When we arrived, we were really pleased to see Halfai and all the elders. We thought they'd invited us there so they could hear more about the teacher. They told me that they've heard reports from the capital that the teacher is not to be trusted and that we should never welcome him back," says Eleazar. Yokkan spits again. "Then I asked them what they believed more – these reports or what they saw with their own eyes. Didn't they see the sick made well? Did the teacher say anything that was against our holy teachings? Halfai told me to be quiet. He said I was young, rude, and ignorant, and that I must listen to those who understand such things."

"Then I asked, 'Where is your authority? Have you ever cured someone of sickness? Does God ever speak through you?'" Yokkan added, with an angry smile.

"That was when Halfai said that we must promise not to speak of the teacher again or invite him to our home. If we didn't, then we would be shunned," says Eleazar. "Then Yokkan said, 'We follow our master and pray that he comes back to our village soon,' and they said, 'Is that your answer?' So I said, 'Of course. We will never stop speaking about him,' and then they told us to get out. So, now we're shunned."

Marta just looks weary at this news, and I chuckle. "Poor Holy Halfai. He can't bear to lose control."

"Miri, it's not funny. What if Yokkan's new carpentry master refuses to keep training him? People have just started greeting us again," says Marta.

"After everything they've seen the doctor do, will people still shun us?" I ask. "And what about people like Ide? Or that shepherd who was cured of his squint? Do you think they'll accept this?"

As it turns out, I'm actually right. Yokkan turns up at

Yokhanan's workshop the next day and is treated exactly the same way as before. Eleazar sees one of his friends near the well and the friend asks loudly when he can come again to hear more about the teacher. Ide and Elisheba, along with many of their relatives, become far more effusive in their greetings than they were before. "Let Halfai cure a few lepers, then he can come and tell me who to shun," says Tauma loudly, having greeted Eleazar outside his stall. This causes a flurry of indignant whispers from the more religious women at the well.

It's now the height of summer; Eleazar helps me bring water up to the olive saplings Father planted. They're established now but I still don't want to risk any of them withering, as they will always remind me of Father. This is the first time we've spent a day together without Marta. We bicker frequently, as we're both stubborn and strong-willed, but it's good-natured bickering. Once the water-skins are empty, we collect firewood, load the donkey up, and carry a bundle each on our backs.

"I'll be honest with you," I say as we trudge homeward. "I never thought I'd like you."

"That's nice to know," he says, with a raised eyebrow and a sardonic smile.

"After Mother died, I think I grew up too fast and you were just my annoying little brother. Then everything happened with Father, and I just started hating you. I just didn't think it would ever be different."

I'm not sure what I expect his response to be, but he just says, "Me too," and then punches my shoulder gently and affectionately.

Now that Eleazar and Yokkan are shunned, they can't join the men at the prayer house on rest day. Instead, we visit Aunt Shiphra's compound. She has an orchard of fig and pomegranate trees, and their kitchen area is shaded by an old vine. Sitting under its green canopy, I look up to see bunches of hard small grapes ripening. We spend the day listening to Yokkan and Eleazar tell us what

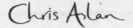

they've learned from the teacher, and recount some of the things they've witnessed.

We're interrupted at one point by an elderly neighbour who is sitting up on her flat roof just out of view. "I can't hear properly," she shouts. "Speak up!"

We invite her to join us and she comes over with her grandson. The next day, as Marta weaves, she intersperses instructions to the apprentices with the stories she heard from Eleazar and Yokkan. They ask shyly if they can come the following week. They bring Elisheba with them. The old neighbour is back with her whole family, and Eleazar's friend joins us, along with his brother. Tauma hears about it from his cousin, Elisheba, and says he'd like to come next week. I see Cured Mariam at the well and invite her and Cyria to join us.

I'm glad we're not meeting in our compound, which would already feel cramped with all these people. I worry for my recovering vegetable patch. Eleazar and Yokkan teach us how to pray the way the teacher does. At the end of our gathering, Eleazar asks us if we want to be hearers of the word, or doers. How are we going to live out what we have learned? We discuss this together.

"Is this how you men discuss things in the prayer house?" Elisheba asks her husband loudly, who has also decided to join us. "Because if it is, you're certainly not a doer."

He smiles ruefully. "No," he says. "This is nothing like what we do in the prayer house."

The week after, our gathering has grown again in size, with most of Elisheba's neighbours attending, along with their husbands and children. We're interrupted by Halfai. He storms into the compound and then pauses, eyeing up each person, as if to say, "I will remember that you were here, and you will regret it."

Once he feels we're suitably intimidated, he lectures us on false prophets and corrupt teachers who spread lies and deception. None of us agree with him, but it's Cured Mariam who interrupts.

"Why are you here?" she asks mildly. "Who appointed you our

teacher? Was it you who cured me? Where is your power? What have you ever taught that has changed even one life?"

We're all stunned, Halfai most of all. Then he recovers. "Cured?" he sneers. "You're as crazy as ever."

Aunt Shiphra clambers to her feet. "Get out of my house," she hisses at Halfai. "You're not welcome here. I shun you. We shun you." There are murmurs of agreement amongst some and fear from others.

"I warn y– " Halfai starts.

"Er, did someone speak?" interrupts Aunt Shiphra. "Certainly no one I care to listen to. Now," she settles herself down on her haunches again, "what were you telling us about the teacher, Eleazar? Please, continue."

Halfai stares impotently for a moment and then leaves, slamming the compound door hard behind him. I've never felt prouder of my aunt, although Eleazar says afterwards that we should forgive Halfai and pray that his eyes will be opened. Yokkan spits hard, clearly unmoved.

Now the village division is official. Each rest day at the prayer house Halfai rants against the charlatan doctor and those blinded by his trickery. Eleazar hears this from one of his friends. "I'm still going to the prayer house every week. I have to or Father will beat me," says one of them, "but in my heart I'm with you."

Despite the weekly sermons against us, numbers continue to grow. Ide starts coming, even though it means she's now shunned by Shoshanna and Imma as a result.

Summer draws to a close and the olive harvest is almost upon us. We need every last olive to make ends meet. If Eleazar and I work from dawn to dusk, and if Marta can take over my water-carrying duties, then we should just about bring in all the olives before the first frost.

"Do you think the apprentices would be willing to help us, just for a few days?" I wonder out loud, squeezing a low-hanging olive.

"It's worth asking Elisheba," says Eleazar, shrugging his robe

Chris Aslan

off and clambering up the tree.

We work hard all day. Eleazar suggests that he beats the olives and I collect them, but I prefer the variety of labour and the satisfaction of knowing I've harvested an entire tree all by myself. We end up with more sacks than the donkey can carry, and leave half a sack nestled under a tree for tomorrow.

"I hope Marta has cooked generous portions," says Eleazar, rolling his olive-spattered shoulders to ease the aching muscles. "I'm hungry, but I'm still looking forward to a swim in the brook more than supper."

We get back and Marta answers the door. By the way her face is lit up, I realize immediately that Malchus is here.

"Any work for a day labourer?" he asks with a smile, as Eleazar runs at him and knocks him over with the ferocity of his embrace. "Don't kill me," he laughs. "And I don't want olive stains on my travelling robe. I told you I'd come back."

Malchus and Eleazar head straight down to the brook. "You go, too," says Marta, presenting me with a nub of soap. "I can finish getting everything ready here. You must be just as tired and sweaty as El."

After we've eaten, Malchus tells us the news. "Opposition to the teacher is growing amongst the religious leaders. I just can't understand it. Why would anyone be against him? We're moving from place to place, never staying in the same house twice, as we've heard rumours that they're trying to arrest him."

"For doing what? Curing people?" I say.

"He cured people on rest days. The holy men are saying it's against the holy law. I know it's stupid. They're jealous and they're afraid of him and of his power."

"We must pray for him," says Eleazar, and then he does. Afterwards, he tells Malchus about our own gathering and the opposition from Halfai.

"It's the same wherever the teacher goes," says Malchus. "Some oppose him and others follow."

Malchus and Eleazar sleep in the covered kitchen area that night, and next morning we head together up to the grove. I can see that Marta wants to go with us, but she knows she can't leave the apprentices alone.

When Malchus takes off his robe, I can't help appreciating how healthy he is, but also how attractive. We harvest olives until midday and then break.

"Why didn't Marta join us?" Malchus asks, cutting the block of cheese into slices.

"She's got her carpet business and her apprentices to think of," I say, "although I know she wanted to be here. She really enjoys your company."

Malchus blushes and busies himself with the cheese. "And I hers," he adds quietly.

If it were any other girl, I'd be jealous, but this is Marta, the most selfless person I know, and I decide that it's time for me and Eleazar to have a little talk about how to help our sister. That evening I clutch my back and ask Eleazar to help me fetch water. We take our time, giving them some moments alone.

"I'm concerned about the harvest," Eleazar says, once we're all eating supper. "Marta, I think we need your help. When the apprentices come tomorrow, tell them that they can have a week off."

The following evening, Marta informs us that the apprentices refuse to stay at home and want to help with the harvest.

This continues for the next few weeks, with rest days spent at Aunt Shiphra's. Malchus teaches us now, and Eleazar and Yokkan are as eager as we are to hear the teacher's new stories and teachings. We take two sacks of olives to Elisheba's in gratitude for the help her daughters have given us.

The harvest is almost finished and I'm wondering what Malchus will do when it finishes. So – I suspect – is Marta. I stay behind on market day to buy salt for the olive brining, and Tauma lends me his camel to transport it back to the compound. I spend most of the morning packing the salt away in the storage room by the stable – not that there's much room amongst the sacks of pomegranate skins and madder root which Marta uses for making dyes. I clean out the olive vats ready for the new harvest. I've been looking forward to some time alone but as I settle down to eat, I find that I'm missing the others and decide to go up and see them.

"Two more trees and we're finished," says Eleazar, beaming, wiping his brow, spattered in olive juice.

I walk over to the tree that Malchus is beating, while Marta collects olives from Eleazar's tree. "So," I say. "Whoever finishes first goes to the brook while the others prepare a celebratory meal."

Marta grins and looks up at Eleazar. "Looks like you'll be eating Miri's cooking tonight."

We race, but this is one thing I can do better than Marta and our tree is finished first. "Come on, Malchus," I say. "We'll see these two later."

We leave them with the donkey and just carry a small sack of olives each.

Finally, I've got him alone. "What will you do now?" I ask. "You know you can stay as long as you want."

"I need to find the teacher again," says Malchus. "When I left, he was talking about his time being almost at an end. I didn't understand what he meant, but it scares me, Mariam. I've got to get back to him."

I pause, choosing my words. "Before we knew about Father's leprosy, there was a man who courted Marta. We thought they'd be married soon, although nothing was official. When Father was cast out, he stopped coming around. As I said, there was never anything official, but it hurt her deeply. He's married now."

"Why are you telling me this?" says Malchus.

"I like you, Malchus. But don't hurt my sister. Don't leave without making it clear what your intentions are."

Malchus flushes red and is pensive. "I know what I would like, but how could she ever want me? She knows what I was."

I laugh and tousle his hair affectionately. "Oh, Malchus, sometimes you can be really stupid. There's not a girl in this village who can keep her eyes off you – including my sister. Why not settle here? You can live with us, start trading dried fish or something."

"You've really thought this through, haven't you?" he grins.

"You really haven't, have you?" I retort. If they do marry, at least one of them will be practical. We near the compound.

"Go," I tell him. "Go to the brook by yourself and think about what you're going to do and what you're going to say. I'll make sure that me and El' are out of your way at some point this evening."

The next morning Malchus prepares to leave. "How will you find the teacher?" I ask.

"It's not that hard. I'll just go to the capital and find out where the latest stories of curing are coming from."

"Tell him to come back soon," says Eleazar. "He promised me that he would."

Marta sighs at the doorway as Eleazar walks with Malchus to the main road. "Thank you. I heard you helped." She turns to me and gives me a squeeze. "I heard that you helped."

She doesn't tell me more, but that's enough for now.

Over the next few weeks, Eleazar and I work hard at brining the olives. We make a good team. He slits each olive, while I replace the brine daily in the completed vats and stir the hot water and salt together until a raw egg floats, which tells me the consistency is just right. We have three stone vats in the storeroom between the stable and our inner room, and soon they're all filled, but we still have olives left. Eleazar borrows donkeys from some of our gathering and loads them up to take the remaining olives to the capital city where they're pressed for oil. He returns with several large jars of oil, which are more than enough for food and lighting.

"We've never had a harvest like it," I say on the evening Eleazar returns. "We won't even need the alabaster jar to pay for the completion of the upper room." Marta looks worried. "What?" I say. "You can't work on your carpets outside in winter, and El needs something to do. Let's finally get the upper room finished."

Yokkan agrees to help Eleazar plane the floors, and Elisheba's husband lends a hand with plastering the walls with adobe, even though it's a little cold in the year to be squelching barefoot, mixing the mud and straw. Once the adobe has had a week to dry, they whitewash everything. I'm kept busy cooking for the workmen. Eventually the room is ready. Marta waits until her current carpet is finished before moving her loom upstairs, tying the warp threads to sturdy posts that Yokkan has purpose-built. We don't have the money to pay for all this yet, but we will in midwinter when we start selling the brined olives.

The apricot tree is bare and the nights cold. Eleazar starts helping Yokkan and Yokhanan, his master. It's not what he wants to do, but he needs to do something. Marta teaches me to use the drop spindle. I'm a little clumsy at first and the yarn I spin is lumpy as a result, but I gradually get the hang of it and discover that I can spin while walking around the compound, which is far preferable to sitting at a loom, and the exercise keeps my legs from getting too cold.

We continue meeting at Aunt Shiphra's each week, wrapped in quilted robes and shawls. Halfai continues to preach against us, but things have calmed down and most people stay more in their own compounds during the chilly winter months. It snows a few times, but the winter isn't too harsh. I see Imma near the well. She's pregnant now and waddles with her hand on the small of her spine. She still ignores me.

Twice a month, Eleazar and I ladle olives out of one of the vats and drain them, put them in sacks and then sell them to traders.

Another carpet is finished, and Marta decides to teach the apprentices and me how to dye wool. Soon dripping wool skeins of red and yellow festoon the bare branches of our apricot tree. Marta decides that Sholum is now ready to start her own carpet.

By the time Sholum completes her first carpet, the apricot tree blossoms. It's a year since the earthquake. Life has taken on a steady and fairly predictable rhythm. I ask Marta when Malchus will return, but she doesn't know. Then one afternoon, Yokkan hammers at the door and suddenly everything changes.

"Fetch Mother," he says, tugging someone else's donkey inside the compound. Yokhanan follows to the side, trying to keep Eleazar upright. Eleazar is sprawled across the donkey, unconscious.

"What happened?" I say.

"Just go," Yokkan snaps, so I do.

At Aunt Shiphra's compound she asks me what his symptoms are, but I don't know. "Mara, stay here. Miri, if I need anything else, you will come back for it."

We hurry back to the compound. The men have carried Eleazar into the inner room. Marta is lighting all our lamps and brings in a clay bowl of glowing coals to warm up the room.

"Stand back," says Aunt Shiphra, taking charge. She feels Eleazar's forehead and then prods his chest and his sides. "Boil me water. Quickly," she says, and Marta and I almost collide in our eagerness to be of some use. Shiphra emerges with a small pouch of powdered willow bark, which she shakes into the water. I glance behind her. Yokkan cradles Eleazar's head with a tenderness I've never seen before. Yokhanan joins us.

"I'm not sure there's anything else I can do," he says. We ask what happened. "Everything was fine. It was just another working day. Eleazar seemed a bit tired, so I told him to sit down and rest for a while. Then he just keeled over. Yokkan said this happened once while they were away and that it was serious. So, here we are."

We thank him and he leaves.

"I remember all those summer fevers he got as a child, but this is different," says Shiphra.

I go into the inner room. "Yokkan, apparently this happened to Eleazar before, when you were away?"

Yokkan nods and tries not to let us see that he's crying. "It was bad, Miri," he says. "Some of the other insurgents were saying that we should just leave him, and that he compromised our safety. I think Shimon was almost convinced, but then someone mentioned the doctor who was nearby, so we slung him on a donkey. By the time we got to the village, I wasn't even sure that he was still breathing, but the doctor took him by the hand and told him to get up, and then he did."

"This happened when he was little, too, but never this bad. Once the willow bark infusion has cooled a little we can try to make him drink some of it," says Shiphra. She looks tired and defeated. "It will make him a bit more comfortable, but that's all."

"What do you mean?" I say, feeling a sudden rising tide of panic. "He's going to be alright, isn't he? He has to be. Aunt Shiphra?"

She ignores me and takes hold of her son with both hands. "Yokkan, my boy, you listen to me. You run. Run without stopping and get to the capital. Find out where the teacher is, then go and tell him to come here immediately. We haven't got much time."

Yokkan glances at Eleazar and is about to bolt through the door, when Marta stops him and gives him a pouch of coins and Eleazar's winter cloak to wear over his robe.

"Now go!" Shiphra says.

She turns back to Eleazar. I draw nearer and can feel heat radiating off him, but he isn't sweating.

"I don't understand," I say to no one in particular. "He was fine this morning. How can this be?"

Chapter Twelve

I don't know what to do with my hands. I've scratched my wrists raw and now they've begun to bleed. I'm up on the roof, pacing. Every now and then I crane my head to see if I can make out any movement on the main road. It's a stupid gesture, firstly because the trees are in blossom and obscure the view down to the main road and secondly, it's only been a couple of hours since Yokkan left. Even if he ran all the way to the capital and the teacher happened to be there, and if the teacher then borrowed a horse to ride out here, he still wouldn't arrive before sundown. That still doesn't stop me craning my head. At least it gives me something to do.

I climb down the ladder past the empty upper room to see if I can help Aunt Shiphra and Marta tend Eleazar.

"Is there any change?" I ask.

"Stop asking all the time," Marta sighs. "If there is we'll let you know."

Aunt Shiphra lifts Eleazar's head onto her lap and then spoons tiny quantities of willow bark infusion into his mouth.

"Will it help him?" I ask. I seem to be good at asking stupid questions.

Alabaster

"Perhaps a little," says Aunt Shiphra, without looking up.

I climb back up to the roof but stop in the upper room on the way to collect my drop spindle and some wool; it'll give my hands something to do other than scratching.

I pace and I spin – craning my head towards the main road every now and then. The yarn is useless, overspun, and keeps crimping. I crane. I try praying, but all I can manage is a repetition of "Bring the teacher, bring the teacher, bring the teacher."

And anyway, which of my wishes should God listen to? For years I wished my brother dead. I remember praying that he would have a long and drawn-out end. Is this all my fault? I drop the spindle and start scratching myself again; harder this time.

I pace. I crane. I scratch. Spots of my blood criss-cross over the roof. I don't notice the sky darken. Eventually Mara comes to fetch me for supper.

"Oh, Mariam," she says, and helps me down the ladder. "What have you done? Let me put some salve on that."

"It's my fault," I mutter. "I hated him and wanted him dead."

"Mariam!" Marta, emerging from the lamplit inner room, sees the bloodied sleeves of my tunic, which are sticking to my wrists. "Don't you think we have enough to worry about?"

"It's my fault. I'm killing him. It's me." Just speaking the words aloud makes them seem more true and I have an overwhelming urge to climb back up on the roof and hurl myself off. "It's me," I keep muttering. I feel something building up inside me. I let it come and the next thing I know, I'm screaming and hitting myself and scratching my face. Mara tries to restrain me and then Aunt Shiphra comes and slaps me as hard as she can across the face, doing the other side for good measure. The pain feels good and it shakes the madness from me.

I slump and let her lead me to the kitchen area, where she hands me a bowl of soup. It tastes medicinal and whatever is in it, I start to feel drowsy. "Come, my peach," she coos, and lays me down on a sleeping mat beside the clay oven. I lie down and fall asleep.

176

Chris Aslan

I wake up groggy with a square of sunlight shining on my face. It's late and I look around, wondering if the teacher has come while I've been asleep. Mara comes out of the stable where she's been feeding the donkey. "How are you feeling?" she asks gently.

My wrists hurt, but that's to be expected. "I'm fine," I say, rubbing my face and trying to shake the grogginess. "Has the teacher come?" She shakes her head. "Is there any change?"

"Marta and Mother are with him," she says, pointing to the inner room and evading my question.

I get up, but then have to sit down again. Whatever Aunt Shiphra gave me hasn't fully worn off. Mara offers me a bowl of cold water, which I drink, and then I enter the inner room.

Lamplight dances around us, filling the air with the smoky tang of olives. This doesn't mask the other smell, though. It smells of sickness in here. Marta is slumped beside Eleazar, holding his hand. I think she's fallen asleep. Shiphra cradles Eleazar's head in her lap, whispering words of comfort and wiping his brow. She looks up. "How are you feeling?"

As if that matters. "How is he?" I ask.

She smiles sadly. "He's not struggling or fighting. It won't be long now. Is there anything you want to say to him? Before..." She trails off.

"Before what?" I feel my eyes fill with tears. "Auntie Shiphra, we can't lose him now, not when we've only just got him back and things are finally right between us."

"Oh, my peach," she sighs.

"It's still not too late. The teacher will get here in time, even if it's at the last moment. I know he will."

My aunt's face twists in grief. "It needs to be now," she whispers, her voice thick with emotion. "We're almost out of time."

"Can I?" I move over to her and she lifts Eleazar's head carefully, and I position it in my lap. It's unnaturally hot and dry. I smooth his hair and I weep. Shiphra leaves me with him.

"Eleazar," I say, trying to speak through the sobbing. "Please

177

hold on for just a little while longer. The teacher is coming. You have to hold on." I swallow and then, remembering what Aunt Shiphra said about saying any last words to him, I continue. "I take back every ill thought, every time I've held hatred and resentment towards you in my heart. I'm so sorry, El. If I could trade my life for yours right now, I would."

My tears splash onto his face and I wipe them with a cloth Shiphra gave me.

"Oh God," I cry out. "Please don't let him die. You know how much the teacher loves him and you listen to whatever the teacher asks of you. Send the teacher now. Quicken his feet, show him the way. Have mercy on my brother who loves you."

We call out together and our voices have power. It almost feels as if God himself enters the room. "Have mercy because you are good, O Lord, and not because we deserve it," I declare. Our voices interrupt and blend together, weaving a prophetic song. I don't know how long we kneel together over our brother and pray like this. Then light floods the room and I think it must be an angel from God or that the teacher has arrived at the last hour.

It's neither. Aunt Shiphra has opened the door and the morning sun slants through it. She comes over and takes one look at Eleazar.

"You can stop your praying now, girls," she says gently. "I've brought salt and a shroud."

We both look at her in confusion. I feel Eleazar's forehead and it does feel cooler, and for a moment my heart soars with hope that the fever is over, but then Marta begins to keen and I realize that before us is a corpse which has already begun to turn grey.

Chapter Thirteen

I sit at our weekly gathering in Aunt Shiphra's compound. The vine above us is covered in little clusters of new leaves beginning to poke through the withered dry stems. They were still just buds this time last week, when Eleazar stood before us leading us in prayer. I remember being distracted by the warm spring sun on my face and not paying attention to what he was saying. I didn't know that that would be the last time he would lead us. I didn't realize how I should savour that precious moment.

Two days have passed already since we stumbled home from the tomb, weak with grief. The teacher didn't even make it for the burial. There's no sign of Yokkan either. Maybe Halfai was right about the teacher after all. Why hasn't he come? Why must it be my loved ones who die uncured?

I'm surprised to see all the usual people at our gathering. Surely we should give up on the teacher now. He promised my brother that he would return soon, but he lied. Most of them, including Marta, still cling to hope.

I don't. Hope tires me. Hope means we can't accept what has actually happened. Marta's hope led to a big argument between us over the alabaster jar. I wanted to break it open and anoint our brother properly for his burial. "We never got to use it on Father," I snap. "It's useless just sitting there in Mother's chest."

"No," said Marta firmly, continuing to wrap each of Eleazar's limbs in strips of linen, shaking spices into each fold. "Don't you remember, El told us about the daughter of the holy man who was sick and died? She *died* but he still cured her. He brought her back to life. Father wanted this jar to be for the living, not the dead."

"Why are we still talking about the stupid teacher?" I demanded. "Where is he? He's not here. He's not coming. Look, he could have borrowed horses from someone. He could have ridden all night, but he didn't. He's not coming."

"Yokkan will find him. He promised that he'd come and he will."

I shook my head in disgust, and then Eleazar's friends knocked on the compound door. Their robes were torn and their heads covered in ash. They'd come with a wooden pallet to carry their friend to his final resting place.

I had put hope aside and knew that this was the last time I would be with my brother. I began to keen as I saw the grief-stricken faces of my brother's friends. I tore at my hair and my tunic, throwing dirt over my head, and fell into the arms of neighbours as mourners gathered to lift the rigid body of my brother onto the pallet.

Then Halfai showed up. For a moment I thought he had actually come to do his duty as holy man and accompany the body to the tombs and recite prayers over it. Then I saw the triumphant look on his face.

"Tell me if this isn't the hand of God upon those who've lost their way? Where's their false teacher now? Where is this power they speak of?" he mocked.

He probably would have carried on like this for longer if I hadn't launched myself at him, my hands, well-practised in

180

scratching, aiming for his eyes. He stumbled back as Elisheba and several other women restrained me.

"You see what they're like, the doctor's followers?" he said, trying to recover his composure. Aunt Shiphra bundled him out of the compound before he could say more.

It was Aunt Shiphra who led the prayers as the pallet was lowered beside the open cave. Cured Mariam sobbed into her mother's breast. Ide had come as well, and just stared blankly ahead of her. Marta found me and took me into a fierce embrace. "This is not the end," she whispered. She wasn't even weeping. Almost of its own accord, my neck began to crane, looking around for plumes of dust or some sign that the doctor was on his way. There was nothing. Like I said, hope is tiring.

I should have entombed all hope with my brother as the main stone was rolled into place and sealed with mud to prevent vermin from getting in. Still I craned my neck for him. Still I was disappointed.

I keep trying to kill hope in my heart but it seems lodged and persistent like a splinter beneath a fingernail. It won't leave me in peace to grieve for my brother, but nor do I have the hope that Marta has. I also feel despair and disillusionment. I hadn't realized how much the teacher and all he taught us had affected my life and the choices I was making, but now I don't know what to believe or who to trust.

My thoughts are interrupted as Aunt Shiphra sits down and then Marta stands up. She never usually speaks aloud at our weekly gatherings, and people shift on their seating mats, interested. "Last week El – Eleazar – told us the story of the two sons and the loving father. He told us to think about the two sons over the week so that we could discuss the story again today." She looks so calm. You'd never know she'd just lost her brother, although I can see from the way she clenches her jaw that there's more going on beneath the surface. "But I've been thinking about the father," she continues. "Eleazar told us how the father ran to meet his lost son. But what did he do before that? He went outside and he waited. Every day he sat and waited, not knowing if his son was even alive or would ever come home. He waited in hope. I wait in hope. We wait in hope."

There's a ripple of agreement and one or two people dab their eyes. I admire Marta right now, but I also think she needs to learn when to let go and accept what has happened. It's noon and everyone unwraps their bundles of food to add to the floor cloth. We didn't bring anything, and anyway, I have no appetite.

I pick at some bread, which I dip in cold mint tea until it softens. My throat still feels hoarse from keening and I'm finding it difficult to swallow.

After midday meal, there is a lot of praying. I collect some of the plates as an excuse not to take part, and then curl up beside the clay oven in the kitchen area and nap. Hope has exhausted me.

The next morning, Elisheba comes round early with her girls. "Don't worry, we're not here to weave," she says. "Here. Fresh herb pastries with the first of this year's greens." She whips off the cloth with a flourish and a cloud of steam, and sits down to join us.

I listlessly pick one up, but it's been so many months since I ate fresh greens that after a nibble I find my appetite returning, and I'm soon on my second. There's a knock at the door and Sholum goes to answer it for us. It's Malchus. He's panting and out of breath.

"The teacher's coming," he says as Marta leaps up and runs to him. "Come, meet him on the main road. He's here to see Eleazar."

Marta hugs Malchus and begins to weep.

"Quickly," says Malchus. "You need to come now if you're going to see him alone before the village mobs him."

Marta glances at me. "Miri?" I shake my head. She can go if she wants. I'm eating my pastries. Let the teacher wait for us, we've waited long enough for him.

"Mariam, go with your sister," Elisheba urges. "He's here!"

I take another measured bite and then say, "My brother is in the grave, which is, at least, a step up from my father, whose body has probably been torn apart and fought over by wild dogs. Both of them put their hope in the teacher. Both are dead. Tell me, Elisheba, why should I rush off to the teacher, eh?"

I'm being rude. Elisheba seems about to say something but then doesn't.

"Would you like some tea?" I ask, wiping crumbs from my mouth and getting up to blow on the embers of our stove, feeding it with a few dry twigs to get it started again. Elisheba looks uneasy, but takes the bowl I offer her. "It's dried mint, I'm afraid, although we should have fresh mint again in a week or two."

Some neighbours come by. "We didn't want you to be alone," they say, peering around for Marta. Then Cured Mariam and her mother join us. I make everyone tea. Elisheba tries to make conversation with the women.

Marta returns to the compound, panting heavily. She nods to the women, who stare at her curiously, and calls me over to her. "Miri, please come. The teacher is asking for you."

"Why did he come too late?" I say.

She tries to keep her voice down, but she can't help being excited. "It isn't too late. Do you know what he told me just now? 'I am the rising.' He will bring our brother back from the dead – I know he will. He is the rising. Come."

She waits for hope to rekindle on my face, but it doesn't. Then with a small sigh of exasperation she grabs my hand, dragging me onto the street, and we run. We run down to the well, ignoring the curious stares. It's market day and we run past stallholders setting up. There are sheep for sale everywhere and more stalls than usual because this is the last market day before our biggest religious festival, and those sheep will soon be sacrificed.

We run past boys skimming stones at the brook, past the tree where Father used to meet us and past the spot where Rohel was stoned. I'm beginning to tire. I look up and see the teacher surrounded by a much smaller group than last time. His face is drawn in exhaustion. I scramble to a halt in front of him. I look at his expression of sorrow, and any hope that welled in me as we ran departs like smoke in the wind. It's too late for the teacher to help Eleazar, and somehow Marta has misunderstood him. Look – he's weeping. He came too late; what else can he do but weep?

I collapse at his feet, trying to regain my breath. "You're too late," I say. "If you'd been here my brother wouldn't have died."

Then I just sit in the dust, taking a handful and throwing it over my head. It's over.

"Mariam, take me to him," whispers the teacher. His voice is husky with hurt. What else is there to do? I don't really want to watch him weeping for the friend he loved and could have saved if he'd just come earlier. I don't understand where his power has gone. He looks tired, powerless, and defeated. As we walk, I even begin to doubt whether I saw him cure so many of the sick. It seems he can cure everyone except those I love. For them, he's always too late.

I walk and I begin to weep.

As we make our way along the foothills of the olive groves towards the rocky outcrop littered with caves where we bury our dead, a hand steadies me and I realize that Elisheba has followed me down. We come to our family cave, and seeing the finality of this enormous rock before us, I kneel down, weeping harder, so desperately sad for all the years of hate and estrangement between me and Eleazar; so brief a time of reconciliation and love. My brother is gone. Someone kneels down beside me, weeping. It's the teacher.

I glance back and see a crowd forming behind us. Some of our gathering have moved forward and as they see the teacher cry, they also understand that he has come too late and that there's nothing to be done. They start to cry too. I don't notice Yokkan until he throws himself against the stone and howls. He beats at

Chris Aslan

the rock with his hands, and some of the teacher's apprentices drag him back before he does himself permanent damage.

The teacher gets up and stumbles back, wiping his eyes with his sleeve. "Open it," he says, looking at the stone. His apprentices look at each other with uncertainty.

"Master, he's been in there for four days," says Marta. "There'll be a smell."

"I told you to believe and you'll see the glory of God," says the teacher, his voice filling with power.

Yokkan is the first to chip at the mud seal and then other men join him and they heave the stone, rolling it to one side of the cave entrance. We've all put our sleeves to our noses, bracing ourselves for the stench.

The teacher lifts his head up, addressing the heavens. "Father, thank you that you have always heard me," he cries. "I know you always hear me, but I pray this now for those here so that they believe that it's you who sent me."

There is silence. Our eyes are all fixed on the teacher as he walks towards the darkness of the cave mouth. "Eleazar," he shouts. "Come out!"

I can't breathe; I can't do anything but watch. The teacher stands there, his chest heaving from emotion, and we peer at the darkness. Nothing.

One or two people begin to whisper but are silenced by others. My stomach clutches and I don't know how I feel; mainly a sense of futility, but with a stubborn wisp of hope. Then we gasp as a hand fumbles along the side of Mother's ossuary. The hand is bound in linen strips. Then something stumbles forward into the light. A woman shrieks and faints, and others begin to cheer.

"Take off the face covering," says the teacher. Yokkan tugs at it. It falls, revealing Eleazar's pallid face squinting against the bright sunlight, looking as if he's just woken up.

Marta, Yokkan and I launch ourselves at him at the same time, almost knocking him over as we cling to him, weeping and

185

laughing. The loops of linen cloth moult off him as we kiss him and then grab on to him again, desperate for his touch to assure ourselves that he's not a ghost.

"Take off the shroud," the teacher laughs, and Malchus tugs at it, loosening it until Eleazar is left shivering and covering himself. Yokkan quickly shrugs out of his robe, and once Eleazar has put it on, he kneels and tenderly ties it, weeping unashamedly.

Eleazar looks behind him at the cave. He's disorientated. "Where am I? What happened?" he says.

He doesn't get a reply because his friends rush forward and then he's being carried on their shoulders through the crowd. Everyone shouts, "He's alive, he's alive!"

It's all a bit too much for me; the running, the weeping, the sorrow turned to joy and before that the pastries. I clutch my stomach, turn, and vomit. Elisheba pats me on the back and says with a chuckle, "If you'd only listened to me, my girl! I told you to go with your sister."

When I look up, Eleazar has gone. The crowd have lifted up the teacher onto their shoulders as well, and we see him and the back of my brother bob along in front of us as everyone makes their way back to the village. I feel a twinge of irritation. My brother has just come back to us and I want him all to myself and want to tell the crowd to go and celebrate somewhere else. But this bringing back from death belongs to all of us. It's our miracle, and I remind myself that the gift of life is a gift of another chance, and that there will be many more days that I'll have together with my brother.

I'm emotionally used up, and lean heavily on Elisheba, still feeling queasy, as the crowd moves forward. Someone starts singing one of our holy songs of praise, and then everyone joins in. It's a raucous affair.

Eventually the crowd arrive back at the village. I wonder if we're going back to our compound and crane my head, trying to find Marta. Instead, the crowd carry Eleazar and the teacher up

Chris Aslan

to the well and then to the prayer house. Anyone who wasn't at the tomb soon hears about what happened, and the crowd grows in size and volume. People jostle to touch Eleazar's feet, to catch some of this extraordinary blessing. Stallholders come to the prayer house with food offerings for Eleazar and the teacher, and people dash home to their compounds, emerging with a jar of honey or a bowl of raisins. A makeshift banquet blooms before us. I see Halfai. His eyes widen at the sight of Eleazar. Then he spits and turns away.

I keep looking for Marta and then see her laughing with Yokkan and Malchus. It seems as if everyone is in the square or the prayer house, laughing and clapping. One or two youths are presented with coins by stallholders and dispatched to outlying smaller villages to tell the sick that the doctor has returned.

A crust of vomit has dried on my sleeve. I haven't bathed or changed my clothes since Eleazar became sick and I need some space to think and just want to feel clean. I head back to the compound where the remaining pastries are still fresh. I touch one in amazement; while it was still warm my brother was dead. I'm struck by the immediacy of everything and laugh quietly to myself in amazement.

I wave off the flies and help myself to a few more pastries, grab a nub of soap and a clean tunic and then take the long way round to the brook, skirting the village. I'm alone and relish the cold of the water against my skin. I wash briskly, as the water is chilly. My wrists open and bleed a little in the water. Then, I sit beside the brook surrounded by fresh green reeds and comb the knots out of my hair. When I've finished here, in the tranquillity and peace, I raise my hands and I begin to praise God, thanking him for the teacher and asking him to forgive my unbelief. Eventually I stop praying but remain there for a little while longer, with just this feeling I've never had before.

I'm about to emerge from the reeds when I see Ishmael striding purposefully beside the brook towards the main road. He wears a travelling cloak but there are no sheep with him. Then I see Halfai hurrying behind him, trying to keep up. I wait until they've gone before I emerge.

I drop my dirty tunic off at home and then wander down to the celebrations at the square. One of the women watching from the sidelines turns suddenly and I almost collide with her. It's Imma. We look at each other awkwardly for a moment. Her baby must be due any day now, judging by the size of her.

"I'm glad your brother is alive again," she says.

"Thank you," I say. Annoyingly, my eyes glass over with tears and I rub them away. It seems my brother's not the only one who has come back from the dead, as far as Imma is concerned. "May God make you a happy mother," I add. "Why don't you ask the teacher to bless you and your child?"

Imma smiles shyly. "I'd like to, but between Ishmael and my father…" She beckons me to step back where we can't be heard. "I don't want anyone to see us talking," she whispers. "But you need to get your brother out of here. It's not safe for him or for the doctor. Ishmael and Father have gone to the capital to tell the authorities where the doctor is. They must leave before dawn."

"Thank you." I squeeze her hand.

"You didn't hear this from me," she says, and then she's gone.

I push myself into the throng. The village wedding band has started playing in the main square and women are dancing around the well. I spot Elisheba holding hands with her girls as they dance. The shepherd who used to have a squint, whose name I can never remember, is butchering one of his largest rams for the feast. I scan the square and then see Marta and Malchus laden with sacks, leaving one of the stalls.

"Just in time," Marta smiles and dumps one of the sacks in my arms. "No one expected payment. We've got pistachios, almonds, raisins, dried figs. Everyone will come back to our home once the feast is over, and we'll still need to serve them something."

"Are we going home now?" I ask.

Marta nods. "Is everything alright?"

I shake my head and she understands and asks no more questions until we close the compound door behind us. I explain everything. "We have to warn the teacher."

"The authorities have been trying this for a while," says Malchus gravely. "But each night we stay somewhere different. It's worked so far, but you saw how tired the teacher is. We can't carry on like this. I'll bring him here."

Malchus slips out and I force Marta to sit down and eat a few pastries while I climb up to the upper room and dismantle the looms. She joins me and we start sweeping.

The teacher and Malchus return just as we've laid out our best carpets. I hurry down the ladder and wash their feet. "How did you get away?"

Malchus smiles and says enigmatically, "When the teacher doesn't want to be seen, he isn't seen."

I don't really understand, but lead them to the upper room while Marta prepares tea.

I tell the teacher what Imma told me and he listens. "Tonight I want you to take Eleazar to visit your family up north," he says to Malchus. "You should stay there for a week. That will be enough time, and then it will be safe for you to return."

Malchus nods.

"What about you?" I ask. "Shouldn't you go with them?"

"No," says the teacher. "Tonight I head for the capital."

"But they're trying to arrest you," I say.

The teacher is quiet for a moment and then he turns to Malchus. "Would you mind seeing if the tea is ready?" he says.

Now we're alone and I sense that the teacher wants to explain something to me.

"You know that I could save Malchus, but not your father," he says. I feel tears prick my eyes at this. "I was able to save Malchus because he came to me. I can only be in one place at one time."

"Then why didn't God send more of you?" I ask.

"I'm the only one," he says. "But after I finish what my father wants me to do here, I'll return to him and then I'll send my spirit. I'll be everywhere." He notices my puzzled look. "Like an olive," he explains, but I am still mystified. "It has to fall to the ground or be eaten by a bird until there's nothing left but the seed, and it's from this seed that a new olive tree grows."

"Are you telling me that you have to die?" I ask, and the teacher nods. I swallow. "Isn't there another way?"

He shakes his head sadly. "But, unlike all those sheep for sale in the market today, I'm willing to lay down my life. It's the only way."

I still don't really understand and feel my eyes well with tears. "Will I see you again?"

He shakes his head. "Not like this."

"So tonight will be the last time?" I ask. He nods. "Do the others realize? Do you think they understand?"

The teacher smiles. "I don't think they want to," he says. "I have tried to explain to them. Most of my other apprentices aren't as quick to grasp these things as you."

He has called me his apprentice again, and I feel happy and heartbroken at the same time. Malchus returns and then I hear Marta calling me. As the sun sets, the dry spring air quickly becomes chilly. I'm glad we're not expecting our guests to sit up on the roof tonight. The chill soon ends the spontaneous feast and then I'm busy washing people's feet and carrying lamps and dishes of dried fruit and nuts up the ladder. There are fewer than twenty of the teacher's apprentices here and they all fit in the upper room along with some of Yokkan and Eleazar's closest friends.

Aunt Shiphra and Mara join us and help boil and serve mint tea. For a moment I'm in the kitchen area alone with Marta. She already knows about the plan for Eleazar and Malchus to leave tonight, although we haven't had a chance to tell Eleazar himself yet. I've barely had a chance to speak to him at all, although there'll be time enough.

Chris Aslan

"Miri, why do you look so sad?" Marta asks.

"Marta, he's going to his death," I say. "He told me. He's going to the capital tonight and he knows that he won't leave alive. He's choosing to go. He says he has to let them do it. He has to die, like the sheep being sacrificed, to open the way for us. Then he won't be stuck in just one body or in one place at one time. Or at least, I think that's what he said. I'm not sure I understood everything. Oh, and he talked about olives. He said something like, 'Unless a seed falls to the ground and dies there can't be any fruit.'"

Marta's brow is furrowed deep in thought. I know better than to interrupt her. "Unless a perfume jar is broken, the fragrance cannot be released," she says quietly. She looks up and holds my gaze, waiting to see if I've understood her intent.

"Are you saying what I think you're saying?" I ask, a smile playing on my lips.

"This is the time, isn't it?" She raises an eyebrow. "It was given to us and now we give it to him."

I try to swallow but there's a lump in my throat. "Father would be proud of us right now," I whisper.

We go into the inner room and open Mother's chest, rummaging through the old tunics until we find the alabaster jar.

"It's so beautiful," sighs Marta, tenderly polishing it with a corner of her tunic. "Can you imagine the skill needed to carve something so delicate and fragile without breaking it? You'd think they'd have made it with a stop or a lid or some way of opening it that didn't involve destroying the whole thing."

"The perfume seller in the capital told Father that it was the jar of kings because only a king could afford to break something so precious that could be used only once," I say.

"Then this is for him," says Marta. "Twice he gave us back our brother." She carries the jar out into the kitchen area.

"What is that?" Aunt Shiphra looks with wonder. "Did the teacher give it to you?"

Marta doesn't even hear her, passing me the jar and returning

191

from the storeroom with the heavy wooden mallet she used to stake her loom into the ground.

"Marta, are you sure about this? What about your dowry?" I say.

Marta just grins as she kneels down. "Do you remember how worried we were after the earthquake when we thought the jar might be cracked?" she says, hefting the mallet in her hand. Neither of us could ever have imagined that one day we would wilfully break the jar. "Hold it upright at the base," she says, and takes a practice swing at it.

"What are you doing?" asks Aunt Shiphra in alarm.

"It's our gift," I say, and I look up at Marta. "Now!"

The mallet swings and connects with the top of the jar. A crack works its way down the top and we see a few drops of spikenard bead along it. The scent is heavenly.

"Again, but harder this time," I say, and Marta grunts as she brings the mallet down, cracking the top of the jar straight off and leaving a spatter trail of spikenard up Aunt Shiphra's robe. She gasps in shock and surprise but also in delight at the scent that has been released.

"Quickly," says Marta. "Take it up the ladder before any more spills."

I scurry up with the jar raised, feeling the spikenard dribbling down my hand and wrist and up the inside of my sleeve. It's viscous, like oil.

At the upper room I hurry inside, dripping spikenard all over the carpets, to where the teacher is reclining.

Then I take one of his feet and I pour.

How do I describe the fragrance? I've never smelled anything like it, so I don't know what to compare it to. It's rich and warm and a little heady. For me, it's the smell of him.

The scent fills the room, intoxicating everyone. They're speechless as I kneel before the teacher, taking his other foot in my hands and pouring more spikenard inexpertly through the jagged hole we've made in the jar. Spikenard spills everywhere and I pull off my headscarf to use as a mop. Without my headscarf, my hair falls around me and catches in the liquid, so I use it to wipe his feet as well.

"It's the most precious thing we have," I whisper to the teacher, "apart from our brother." I've just knocked the jar over but it doesn't seem to matter as I think it's empty. "It's not enough, I know, but we want to honour you and to prepare you for what's to come."

"Thank you," says the teacher gently. I feel the healthy solidity of his feet, so sturdy and full of life. This body will soon be broken and destroyed, like the jar. He chooses to do this for us. I fight an overwhelming desire to tell him to run with Eleazar and to save himself. I know he could. I know he won't. I glance up and his eyes are glassed with tears and my heart feels as broken as the jar beside me and I start to weep. I wipe and I weep, whispering my adoration.

I only stop when I hear Malchus say icily, "Let go of her."

One of the teacher's apprentices, looking furious, has grabbed Marta by the wrist. "You stupid girls," he snarls. "Do you even know what spikenard is worth, especially a jar of that size?"

"Yahuda," the teacher warns.

"No! I'm the one who has to keep us all fed. And what about the poor? She should have sold the jar instead of wasting it." He's pointing at me.

"You'll always have the poor with you, but soon I'll be gone," says the teacher. "She's preparing me for my burial." He looks at me. "Miri, this act will never be forgotten. I'm telling you, wherever people follow me they'll hear of this and remember it."

Yahuda still glowers at me, his nostrils flaring. "Guh!" he grunts and then storms down the ladder.

"Thank you," says the teacher, and slowly draws his feet away. He lowers his voice. "Now, take Eleazar out of here before you tell him to leave. There can be no goodbyes," he whispers. I nod, sniffing, and pick up the broken jar and a few shards of alabaster and place them in an alcove beside the lamp. I go over to Eleazar and ask him and Malchus to come down to the kitchen area.

Eleazar has still barely said anything to me. "Some of the apprentices are really angry about the waste," he says to Malchus, and then turns to me and plants a kiss on my cheek. "That was the most beautiful thing I have ever seen in my life," he says.

"You mean 'lives'," I say smiling.

"Is your wrist hurt?" Malchus asks, putting his arm around Marta tenderly.

"It doesn't matter," she says, leaning into him, unashamed.

"I'm proud of you both," says Eleazar, and then frowns. "What did the teacher mean about being prepared for his burial? Everyone saw today; he's more powerful than death."

"El, you have to leave," I say. "It's not safe for you here, or for the teacher. Malchus will explain along the way. I'll tell Yokkan for you. You can't go back up there; the teacher said 'no goodbyes'. You just have to leave now."

Marta has already prepared a bundle with an extra robe, travelling cloak and some dried fruit and nuts, and hands Eleazar a pouch of coins. We hold each other tightly, the three of us. Then Marta kisses Malchus tenderly on the lips, and Eleazar and I exchange a quick smirk. "We'll pray for you," she says, as they slip out of the door.

I put my arm around her.

We're about to climb back up to the upper room, braving the disapproval of those who think we've wasted the jar.

"Let's just go up on the roof for a moment," I say, and we keep on climbing. I'm not sure why I suggested this. It's cold, and my hair and headscarf are still wet with spikenard. "Marta, will you hold my legs still?" I ask. I clamber up onto the wall at the corner, standing tall. Tree blossom still obscures our view of the main road but behind it, as I crane my head, I see the bob of moving torches coming towards the village. There are a lot of torches.

"Quick," I say, spinning round and almost losing my balance. "We have to warn the teacher. They're coming for him."

Chapter Fourteen

The morning sun slants through the window opening into the upper room. In their hurry to leave, someone forgot the cloth belt of their robe, and one of the lamps was knocked over and the oil has stained a carpet. The largest stain is in the middle of Mother's finest carpet where the spikenard soaked in. It's ruined the carpet, of course, or maybe it's made the carpet even more precious to us. The room still smells intoxicating, masking the underlying residual odour of too many unwashed men in a confined space. I still smell amazing, and am loath to ever wash my hair or headscarf again. If I ever have the good fortune to smell spikenard again, it will always remind me of the teacher.

We're meant to be clearing up, but Marta has sat down heavily, and gingerly prods her jaw. She's had less experience with beatings than I have.

"Has the swelling gone down?" I ask her.

"I think he might have knocked a tooth loose," she says, wincing as she probes inside her mouth.

"If there's one thing to be said for my ex-husband, he knows how to throw a punch," I say.

"You can tell he's had practice," Marta says, which makes me grin – a mistake because it stretches my lip, which starts bleeding again. "Seriously, I can't imagine what it was like for you enduring all those beatings alone."

I nod. "But I wasn't afraid at all last night, knowing that you were there, and also that it would take more than a few punches for us to tell them anything."

The previous evening, Yokkan led the teacher and his apprentices around the village, getting to the main road just after Halfai, Ishmael and the other religious leaders blazed up to the well, armed with swords and torches.

We just had time to snuff out all the lamps upstairs before Halfai hammered at the door. When they saw that the teacher had already left and demanded to know where he'd gone, I tried to delay them to give the teacher more time to get away. I mainly just asked questions about who exactly they were looking for and why they wanted to arrest someone who had done nothing but good. Eventually Ishmael lost his temper with me and lashed out, and then, when Marta tried to stop him, she got a few punches as well. If they'd found the teacher we would have heard about it by now. He got away.

Only now as I stare at the depression he left on the cushions against the wall, and the spikenard stain on the carpet, does it really sink in that although his presence is still so fresh, we won't see the teacher again. I feel sad, but I also feel an unexpected sense of peace. I reach down to pick up some of the shards of alabaster I missed last night. "Miri, your wrists," says Marta. I look down at them and the scabs left from where I scratched them have completely gone. When did that happen? "He must have cured you," she says. "How are we going to go back to life like it was before? I can't imagine life without him."

"We won't," I say. "He's coming back, just not in the same way," I say. "Remember what he told you? 'I am the rising.'"

I can't explain it, but I feel that there are things I'm only just beginning to understand about him.

"What should we do with the broken bits of alabaster?"

"I've put them all with the remains of the jar up in the alcove."

Marta goes over to it and peers inside. "You know, there's still some spikenard left inside – just a bit." She lifts the broken jar and inhales it deeply. "We could pour it into something – maybe even sell it."

I come over and peer in, tilting the jar. Then I feel as if the teacher is just behind me and the feeling is so strong that I turn around. There's no one there, but I know what to do with the remaining spikenard.

"Can I have it? There's someone I want us to see."

Marta looks at me quizzically.

"I'd like to visit Shoshanna, Rivka and Imma. I want to pour at least a drop on each foot."

Marta looks baffled. "Imma, I understand; after all, she did warn us yesterday about what would happen. But why Shoshanna? And Rivka's shown you nothing but spite."

"I know," I muse. She's right, of course. But until now I've never thought about why Rivka is so bitter. What made her that way? I think about Shoshanna and how ruled she is by the fear of what others think about her. Then there's Imma. Is she happy with Ishmael? Has he ever laid a hand on her?

"What about Ishmael?" says Marta, unconsciously rubbing her freshly bruised jaw.

I shrug. "Come with me," I say. "They're no less deserving than we were. They need him just as much as we did."

We pick up the broken alabaster jar with the remaining spikenard and leave everything else to tidy up later. I notice the swirls and whorls in the alabaster that used to fascinate me so much as I wondered what the future held. Now I don't need to know.

I don't know why, but I find myself thinking of Mother. I can still hear her telling me what all women in our village tell their daughters: "Mariam, a woman's honour is as fragile and as beautiful as a butterfly's wings. What is a butterfly without wings, except a worm? Remember this. Guard your reputation, for it is more precious even than a husband or sons."

How would she feel if she had lived to see me now? We walk down the street together. One of the elders sees us and spits on the ground in contempt. I am a bad woman; at least, in the eyes of many in our village. And yet I hold my head higher, as I feel that Mother would have told me to do, as I walk on with my sister. I am not a worm. I am a woman and the teacher called me his apprentice. Life might not be any easier than before the teacher came, but it is better. I feel wistful, but more than that, I feel an overwhelming sense of peace; not that everything will be alright, but that I will never have to face it alone.

As we walk back up to the village, my senses are filled with a heady lightness. We pass Cured Mariam, who is anxious to know that the teacher got away safely. She inhales deeply, smiles, and then she's gone. At the well some greet us and others turn their backs. The teacher has brought division to our village. I don't think anyone has been left entirely unaffected or entirely neutral. But even the women who turn to shun us lift their heads and breathe in the scent. They can't help closing their eyes and inhaling the fragrance that still emanates from the broken shards in my hand, from my matted hair, and damp headscarf.

Everything smells of him.

Acknowledgments

I hope you've enjoyed this book. If you'd like to discover the original source material for yourself, it can be found in the biblical accounts of Luke (chapter 10) and John (chapters 11 and 12). You can find them here: www.biblegateway.com

Thanks and apologies to Revd Helen Shannon. Your sermon on the alabaster jar got me daydreaming an origins story, which meant I stopped listening to what I'm sure was a great preach.

Kenneth Bailey's book, Jesus Through Middle Eastern Eyes (SPCK), helped me see that I knew first-century Palestine better than I'd realized and gave inspiration for me to tackle this time period. Thanks to Naures Atto for helping me with the original Aramaic names of the biblical characters and to Richard Bauckham for providing me with contemporary names of that time and giving constructive feedback on the first chapter. I'm also indebted to "the internet" in general, particularly Wikipedia, for helping me with general research.

Thank you, Mum and Dad, for letting me monopolize your dining-room table for a summer, bringing this story to life.

I'm also grateful to Omar Al-Hayat, Cathy Priest, Rosie Edser,

Alabaster

Naomi Morton, Dr Iain Pickett, Dr Tim Campion-Smith, Caroline Titus and Dr Jenni Williams for their helpful feedback, and special thanks to Pat Alexander, Anne De Hunty, Robin Whaley and Emma Goode for helping shape this story.

Thank you, Becki Bradshaw, for being willing to read this manuscript even though you're the non-fiction commissioning editor at Lion Hudson, and many thanks to my editor, Jessica Tinker, for her encouragement and commitment, polishing the manuscript and getting this story out there. Thanks also to Sarah J. Coleman for creating such a great front cover, and to Sheila Jacobs, for her attention to detail.

And lastly, hello to Jason Isaacs.

Author's Note

Today, leprosy, although easily cured, continues to hold such a negative stigma that often those who discover a white patch on their skin hide it rather than seek treatment, fearing ostracism and rejection from their communities. The term "leper" has become a pejorative. If you would like to find out ways you can help those with leprosy, please contact: www.leprosymission.org.uk

Next from Chris Aslan:

Manacle

… coming soon from Lion Fiction!

Also from Lion Fiction:

The Abbess of Whitby

· ·

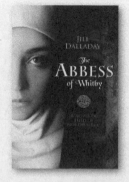

"This is skilful and accomplished writing."
– Peter Tremayne, author of *The Sister Fidelma Mysteries*

· ·

SHE WILL FORGE A
NEW BRITAIN

Hild is caught between two worlds. Handmaid to the goddess
Eostre, she finds herself tossed from one power to another – the
indifferent goddess, the callous King, her crass husband – before
meeting the Christian priests of Iona and finding a home for her
bruised spirit.

Then the young convert catches the eye of Aidan, a charismatic
leader. Inspired and guided by him, she builds communities,
creates trust, leads men. Even her old enemy, King Oswy, entrusts
his child to her, and seeks her help to heal his divided kingdom.

A woman of power and wisdom, subtle and brilliant, she will
change the history of her nation.

· ·

ISBN: 978 1 78264 154 4 | e-ISBN: 978 1 78264 155 1

THE BOY WHO LOVED RAIN

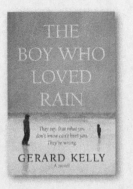

"A compelling debut novel... combines elegance and passion."
– Derek Wilson, historian and novelist

The anger runs deep; from some untraceable darkness;
and it is stealing his will to live.

Colom had the perfect childhood, the much-loved only child of a
church pastor. Yet he wakes screaming from dreams in which his
sister is drowning and he can't save her.

Fiona turns to her husband, desperate to help their son. But
David will not acknowledge that help is needed – and certainly
not help from beyond the church.

Then they find the suicide pledge.

Fiona, in panic, takes Colom and flees... but when will she
acknowledge that the unnamed demons Colom faces might be of
her and David's own creation?

ISBN: 978 1 78264 129 2 | e-ISBN: 978 1 78264 130 8